TOMORROW

Seemingly with inside help, three men break into the laboratories of Atomic Power Inc., killing three guards and stealing a new formula for the control of atomic fission. However, the intruders are caught on camera, and one of them bears the dark streak of an indelible brand across his forehead — the debtor's mark! Private investigator Jim Carter knows that mark well, but in accepting the case to share the reward money with his informant — he's already marked for death . . .

E. C. TUBB

TOMORROW

Complete and Unabridged

LINFORD
Leicester

First published in Great Britain

First Linford Edition
published 2012

British Library CIP Data

Tubb, E. C.
Tomorrow.- -(Linford mystery library)
1. Suspense fiction.
2. Large type books.
I. Title II. Series
823.9′14–dc23

ISBN 978–1–4448–1258–9

Published by
F. A. Thorpe (Publishing)
Anstey, Leicestershire

Set by Words & Graphics Ltd.
Anstey, Leicestershire
Printed and bound in Great Britain by
T. J. International Ltd., Padstow, Cornwall

This book is printed on acid-free paper

1

Tomorrow

It was one of those days. I felt it when I jerked awake to the trilling of the videophone, and when I saw Branscome's face I was certain of it. He glowered at me, his flickering image streaked and marred with the trails of radioactive particles blown from the mainland, and I twitched with unconscious reflex action to the mind-disturbing radiation from the wind-blown debris.

'Carter?'

'What do I look like?' I stared at him, at his flabby cheeks coated with stubble, his red eyes, and the long hair straggling over his dirty neck. A cigarette hung from the corner of his mouth and when he spoke I could almost smell his breath.

'Hell,' he said, and spat out the butt. 'Get down here as quick as you can.'

'Why? A job?'

'Yeah. Tell you more later. Hurry now.'

The flickering screen died and I leaned against the cool plastic trying to ease the throbbing of my head. I felt irritable, the same as I always did when the wind blew over the deadlands, and I hated the very thought of obeying orders. This was a free world, had been since the Blowup, and a man did what he wanted when he wanted, and how he wanted. That was freedom and I was free.

But I still had to eat.

Someone in the next apartment had a radio going at full blast and the thudding of the downbeat vibrated through the thin walls. I tried to ignore it, shaving carefully around the edges of a half-healed knife slash down one cheek and watching the percolator at the same time. I failed in both efforts, the coffee bubbled over the stove, and a thin rill of blood ran from where I had caught the wound.

I cursed, hammered on the wall and refilled the percolator. While it was heating I staunched the flow of blood and finished my dressing, trying to figure out what Branscome had lined up for me.

I chose my best and cleanest slacks and blouse, black with yellow piping, tucking the tops of the slacks into knee-boots of black leather. A short jacket and a visored cap of stiffened nylon coloured to match, completed my attire. I slipped on heavy signet rings and checked the loading of the gun before slipping it into a concealed holster, and by that time was ready for breakfast.

The pounding of the radio seemed to be getting louder, making it hard to think straight, and when the coffee boiled over for the second time I'd just about had enough.

Ringing the doorbell didn't work, and knocking was a waste of time. It wasn't until I had almost kicked the door from its hinges that I got results and by that time the corridor was full of curious heads sticking out from opened doorways.

I ignored them, staring at the man who had opened the door.

He was a big, sweaty, beefy-looking man with truculent eyes and a battered face. I had seen him once or twice around town, a promoter of mixed fights with a share in one or two happy-smoke joints. A man with friends, which made him a man to be careful of — unless, of course, his friends were of the usual kind.

He stood glaring at me, a cigarette smouldering between his lips and a half-full bottle in one hand. The room behind him was full of smoke and stank of stale liquor and the heady scent of marijuana.

'Wattya want?'

'The radio. Turn it down.'

He didn't move, just stood staring at me through the smoke of his reefer. The thudding of the radio boomed along the corridor and I could feel the staring eyes belonging to the heads sticking out into the passage.

'Look,' I said patiently. 'I live next door and I can do without sound effects, so how about turning down your radio?'

'Go to hell,' he said without emotion. He stepped back ready to slam shut the door, then stopped as he saw where I'd put my foot.

'Do you turn it down, or do I do it for you?'

He stared at me, his eyes hot and glittering and the knuckles of his hand whitening as he tightened his grip on the bottle.

I beat him to it.

The heel of my palm smacked his chin, sending him staggering back from the door. I took three long strides into the room, jerked the cable from the power socket, tore off the plug and threw it into the lap of a blonde sitting vacuously in a deep chair. Three more strides and I was back in the corridor ready to forget the whole thing.

He had other ideas.

A yell warned me. One of the staring heads had opened its mouth and called a warning, which one or why I neither knew or cared. I ducked, spinning on one heel, facing back down the passage and ready for action.

He came at me with his mouth open, his eyes glittering with hopped up rage, and a knife in his hand. I could have disarmed him. I could have jerked aside and smacked him down. I could have done a lot of things, but I was fed up and irritable.

I shot him three times in the body.

* * *

Branscome waved me to a chair as I entered the office, and pushed a box of cigarettes towards me. I helped myself, wishing that I dared to fill my pocket, but knowing that if I did he'd cut the rate on whatever job he had to offer, and I needed money.

'What kept you?' he snapped irritably. 'I told you to get here quick.'

'I had trouble, shot a man and had to clear up the mess. What have you got for me?'

'Anyone I know?' He narrowed his eyes as he stared at me. I shrugged.

'Some jerk who used to own a loud radio. Forget it. What's the job?'

'The usual.' He ran dirty fingers through his lank hair and tossed a paper towards me. 'Recovery job. Atomic Power Inc.'

'Yes?'

'Someone broke into their laboratories last night, killed three guards and stole a new formula. They blame the Antis.'

'Why should they?' I picked up the paper and ran my eye over the usual list of suspects. 'Couldn't it be a commercial theft? What would the Antis want with a secret process?'

'How would I know,' he snapped. 'It's on general circuit, all the agencies will be on the lookout for the thief. You've got to get to him first.'

'What terms?'

'The usual. Five thousand on delivery.'

I shook my head, dropping the paper back onto the desk. 'What are you giving me? Atomic Inc. would pay more than that for what they want. If they've called in all agencies it must be important otherwise their own people would handle it.'

He sighed, staring at me without anger, picking at his grimed fingernails. 'If you wasn't about the best operator in town I wouldn't argue with you,' he said. 'You know how things are with me, I can't even afford to hire regular personnel.' He threw the paper back at me. 'Alright, then, we split two ways. You pay your own expenses. Right?'

I nodded, it was the best I could hope for.

'Good. The thieves broke in about two in the morning. There must have been at least three of them, and they stole the guards' weapons so now they are armed. I think they were freelancing, they may try to contact Fission Products, or one of the other companies, but the big agencies will have them covered so that narrows our field.'

'That doesn't help much. It could be a freelance job, but I doubt it. They would need inside help, someone must have given them the guard schedule and a plan of the laboratories. If there is big money in this I'm stuck.'

He nodded, pulling at his cuticles. 'Maybe there is something in this Anti scare,' he said slowly. 'Atomic Inc. seem to think so, and they should know.' He glared at me with sudden heat. 'Well? Get moving on the job or do I get another operator?'

I grinned and helped myself to his cigarettes. What he thought didn't matter now. I was on the job.

It was cold outside, mid-winter cold, and the wind brought a promise of heavy snow. I shivered a little, turning up the collar of my jacket and tried to think out the next move. First I had to scan the issued report, then get on the trail of whoever it was had stolen whatever it was from some of the best guarded premises in the world.

Simple.

I sighed and entered a coffee house, stepping over the sprawled forms of beggars whining outside. A girl came up to take my order, a tall, well-made girl with makeup, which did a good job of disguising her mottled skin. I ordered coffee and flapjacks, and while waiting for the food scanned the report.

I was lucky. Spy cameras had caught the thieves, and one of them had forgotten to shield his face. He wore rags and had a thick growth of stubble, but what caught my eye was the dark streak across his forehead. I knew that brand!

Knew it too well! The debtors' mark, and that immediately narrowed the field of search.

I chewed the food, trying not to notice the taste of soy, and gulped the tepid coffee, staring at the paper spread before me on the table. The debtors' mark couldn't be removed. Couldn't! He had owed money, had been tracked and caught, forced to work off his debt, and then been branded as a warning to others. Such men weren't wanted, they were outcasts, pariahs, lower even than the beggars. I smiled as I looked at the tell-tale mark, then looked up with sudden suspicion.

The waitress stood at my shoulder staring down at the paper.

* * *

It was almost dark by the time I got back home. A thin drift of sleet fell from the lowering clouds, settling on the buildings and being churned into freezing slush in the streets. Few people were abroad, those that were either couldn't help it or were out on business and none of them seemed interested in me.

I stepped into the foyer, flashing my identification at the house-guard. He touched his cap and operated the electric lock permitting me to enter the building, and I crossed the foyer to his booth.

'Any messages?'

'No.' He stared at me from beneath the visor of his cap. 'Some people were asking after you, your ex-neighbour must have had a lot of friends.'

'What of it?' I shrugged and lit a cigarette. 'Did you take care of him for me?'

'Yes, the cremation and other fees will be on your bill.' He hesitated and I looked sharply at him.

'What's the matter? Didn't you like the idea of my killing him?'

'It's nothing to me what you do, but we don't want trouble. Next time do your killing outside the building, it saves a lot of work.'

I grinned and dropped a bill into his lap. He didn't move, and I shrugged and turned towards the elevator. Some people were peculiar, and I wondered what it must have been like in the old days. I stepped out at my floor, not bothering about the extra clean spot in the passage, and slipped a key into my lock.

I had entered the apartment before I knew that something was wrong, and when I did, it was too late.

A man sat in my easy chair, a gun in his hand and the tiny orifice pointed straight at my stomach. A second man stepped from behind the door, and relieved me of my own pistol, while a third stood just within the bathroom. I stared at them, then shrugged and leaned against the wall.

'What is all this for?'

'Don't you know?' The man in the easy chair twisted his lips in what he must have thought was a smile. I didn't like the look of his teeth. 'The man you shot this morning was a friend of ours, now do you know?'

'You've come to thank me,' I guessed. 'I didn't like him either.'

'Smart guy,' said the man at my right, and smashed the edge of his hand across the bridge of my nose. 'Shall I give it to him, boss?'

'Wait.' He rose from the chair and stood in front of me. I tried not to look at his rotting teeth. 'Listen you, maybe I didn't like that man much either, but unless we do something about it what's to stop some other smart operator drilling us?' He shook his head, and I almost felt sorry for him.

'It's a hell of a world,' I said. 'Now either give it to me or get the hell out of here. Your breath stinks.'

He turned white, his skin glistening over his cheekbones and the pupils of his eyes dilating with sheer rage. He swallowed, licking his lips and half-raising his gun.

I kicked him in the groin.

Before he dropped I had turned and driven the fingers of my right hand into the eyes of the man who had broken my nose. He screamed, doubling forward, his hands flying to his face. I chopped down at the base of his neck, feeling the vertebrae snap beneath the blow, and dived for my gun as the man in the bathroom opened fire.

He was a lousy shot, or maybe he was worried about hitting his boss, and he had loosed three times before I was ready for action. Something whined past my ear and something burned into my left arm leaving it limp and useless. The groaning figure of the man with the bad teeth jerked and was silent. I rolled, ignoring the pain from my arm and concentrating on the man in the bathroom. He must have thought that he'd hit me, or perhaps he was just naturally careless. He stuck his head past the edge of the door for a better view, and I shot him neatly between the eyes.

For a moment I lay on the ruined carpet, feeling the pain of my broken arm, and wondering if my face was fit to be seen. Footsteps pounded along the passage, and someone hammered on the door.

'Come in,' I yelled, 'it isn't locked.'

It swung open and I grinned at the startled face of the house-guard. I must have been a little lightheaded from the pain of my wounds, or perhaps it was just the reaction from a busy day but suddenly everything seemed extremely funny.

I was still laughing when the lights went out.

* * *

The surgeon clucked like an old woman as he saw my arm. He washed the blood away with alcohol and tightened his lips as he felt around the wound, his eyes tired and strained looking

'What's the matter, Doc?' I reached for a cigarette with my good arm and shivered a little in the chill of the hospital receiving ward. 'Is it bad?'

'Could be worse.' He frowned at the cigarette. 'Pistol?'

'Yes. It would have blasted my arm off if I hadn't been wearing a metallic lined jacket, the gunner had a H.V. job'

'You were lucky.' The surgeon reached for a pad of blanks. 'What treatment can you afford?'

'The best I hope.' I frowned at the fluorescents in the ceiling. 'What would it cost?'

'Normal setting, splints, plaster cast and three X-rays will come to a thousand. Staders come to four thousand.' He hesitated, his pencil poised over the pad. 'If you can't pay you can have charity, or if you don't want that you can work it off over a period.'

'Staders,' I decided. 'I've got to keep working.'

He shrugged and put down the pad. 'Can you pay?'

I dug money from my pocket. The three goons had each carried a fair roll, but it still fell short by five hundred. I looked at the surgeon.

'Will you take a cheque?'

He nodded, and wheeled a videophone over to the couch. I dialed the bank and he spoke to the cashier.

'Jim Carter, account number . . . ?' He looked at me and I told him.

'Account number one seven zero five three four. Is he good for five hundred?'

The cashier made a check of his screen, then nodded. 'Yes. Do you want a transfer?'

'One moment,' I said. I scribbled the

cheque and stuck my thumb onto the prepared surface. I held the slip over the scanners, and in the vision screen I saw the cashier nod as he compared the print with the one he had on his screen.

'Satisfactory. Which account?'

'Medical. Two five nine seven.' The surgeon waited for the acknowledgment and killed the screen. He nodded towards a nurse, and began to wash his hands.

'Prepare the patient for Staders, nurse. Local anaesthetic.'

It was soon over.

* * *

The sleet had given away to snow and the thick white flakes swirled in a bitter wind as I stood on the steps of the hospital and thought out my next move. My arm was still numb from the anaesthetic, and would be sore for several days while the incisions healed, but I could use it and that was the important thing. I flexed my fingers and worked the muscles as I stood shivering in the night

A kiosk stood at the comer, a barred

metal pillbox with a wire mesh grill and a solitary attendant. I strode up to it fumbling in my pockets for money.

'Cigarettes. Five cartons.'

'Tobacco or marijuana?'

'Tobacco.' I slid money beneath the plastic front and received my change and five cartons. I tucked them beneath my left arm and bumped into a soft something as I turned away.

It was a man, boy rather, a loose-limbed, gangling idiot-faced hophead with a shock of wild hair and a deathly white face. He clutched at my arm, the bad one, and I winced beneath his grip.

'Help me, mister,' he whined. 'Gimme a shot, just the price of a single shot. Honest I ain't had any since I don't know when. Please mister. Please.'

Any other time and I would have short-armed him away from me, but this time was different. I had a damaged arm, a job to do, and perhaps I may have even felt a little sorry for the guy. I nodded, and thrust a bill into his claw-like hand. He whined like a dog with eagerness as he hurried to the booth and received his bundle. He stood in the street, the snow whipping about his rags and settling on his shock of hair — and sniffed his paradise.

The cocaine took almost instant effect, it always does on an empty stomach, and I watched as he smiled in the grip of drug-induced euphoria.

'Thanks, mister,' he said with simple dignity — and stepped from the sidewalk straight into the path of a passing car.

It didn't stop, of course, and when I left, the beggars were already fighting over possession of the body.

I couldn't blame them. After all the man was dead, and the rags would probably fetch the price of a meal.

* * *

Someone had once said that the edge of town was a model of Hell, and sitting in the darkness, my back to a wall of shattered concrete, I could well believe it. Around me the ruins sprawled in a jumble of twisted metal and shattered stone. Weeds grew thickly in the crevices, dead now, their once sickly green leaves covered with snow, and the ethereal blue of the deadlands threw a faint luminescence over the deserted sector.

I turned up the collar of my jacket, wishing that I'd had the sense to buy a cloak when I'd had the money, and settled even closer against the poor shelter of the ruined concrete.

I sat and smoked and thought. I sat and smoked, and sometimes just sat and thought, and in the end I just smoked. It grew colder, the wind-driven snow lashing at me with icy fingers, drifting down my neck and making my arm throb with a dull agony.

I began to get cramp and I would probably catch a cold but still I sat and smoked and thought.

I couldn't do anything else.

He came at last. He came when I was almost paralysed and frozen. He came in a swirl of snow, a shadow among shadows, sitting beside me a shapeless lump in the blue-limned darkness squatting on his haunches and oblivious to the snow covering him with a film of white.

Silently I handed him the cigarettes, silently he took them, tearing open a package and slipping one of the little white cylinders between his lips. Silently he struck a light.

I didn't scream. I had seen him before and even if I hadn't I still wouldn't have expressed either horror or disgust. He couldn't help it. No man could help a face that wasn't a face, eyes that weren't human eyes, a body that couldn't wear normal clothing. Life was bad enough for him without my making it worse.

But I was glad it was dark.

He smoked for a while in silence, the tiny red coal of his cigarette brightening and dimming as he inhaled the nicotine-loaded fumes.

I smoked with him, chain-smoked, lighting one cigarette from the butt of another, trying to steady the quivering of my hands. Time crawled past and still we sat in silence.

'Trouble?' His voice was a whisper coming through the darkness like a flake of snow, gentle and light and unexpectedly warm and human.

'I am looking for a man who stole a paper from a guarded laboratory,' I drew on my cigarette and stared at the glowing tip. 'A branded man, or perhaps just a man who wore a brand. You know him?'

'No.'

I wasn't disappointed, it had been a faint hope and a thin one, but I didn't move from where I sat. He sighed a little as he sucked at his cigarette, and now it was my turn;

'Trouble?'

'It will be a hard winter,' he said. 'I doubt if there will be many of us left to greet the spring.'

'Is that bad?'

'No.'

Again we sat in silence, smoking and thinking, the red coals of our cigarettes warm and human in the wind and snow and desolation.

'There are those who may have what you seek.' His voice seemed utterly disinterested, a thin whisper against the rising wind.

'The Antis?'

'Yes. They would want it, they seem to

want many strange things.'

'Do you know if they have it?'

He shrugged, the snow flaking from his hunched shoulders as he moved. I tried again.

'Has it left the city?'

'No.'

We sat for a while in silence, then he touched the cartons of cigarettes.

'Take them.' I rose stiffly to my numb feet, shaking the snow from my jacket, and trying to beat feeling into frozen fingers.

'Goodbye.'

'Goodbye — son,' he whispered.

When I looked back he was gone.

I was so cold that it was hard to think straight, and the first need was coffee and food. By chance I entered the business and residential section of the city near the coffee house with the curious waitress, and didn't tread on more than a couple of beggars as I entered the place.

It was warm inside, and a little crowd had gathered around the television screen watching seven girls dance to the wail of pipes and the throb of drums. I sat at the same table and watched her as she crossed towards me.

'Coffee and a plate of ham and eggs.'

She didn't make the obvious answer, just stood patiently waiting until I learned some sense. Her makeup had worn thin and her mottled skin didn't look too good at close quarters.

'Coffee and a bowl of energised soup.' I smiled apologetically at her, turning on the charm. She frowned.

'Bread?'

'Please.'

The dancing girls had left the screen and the crowd hunched closer as the main event of the evening flashed on. She returned with the food and I gestured towards the crowd.

'Do you go for the fights?'

She shrugged, setting the bowl of thick soup before me and putting the coarse bread beside it. I caught her arm.

'Listen, don't get me wrong, but I'd like to know you better than I do. What time do you finish?'

'In thirty minutes.'

'Will you come out with me?'

She hesitated, staring down at me, but I

wasn't worried. I knew what the answer would be.

'Yes,' she said. 'I'll meet you outside.'

I grinned over my soup.

The thirty minutes passed and I waited outside the coffee house, stamping my feet in the freezing snow. She came as I knew she would, and I hailed a fleet cab passing in the street. It pulled up with a spray of snow, and the cabbie stared at me through his wire mesh.

'Where to?'

'Marino's.' I heard the click of the lock and ushered her into the cab just as the beggars began to gather around us. I ignored them, settling back in the warm darkness suddenly conscious of her nearness. It troubled me, women usually didn't affect me that way.

Marino's was a happy-smoke joint, which also promoted select fights on the side. She obviously wasn't used to such places, and stood just within the foyer pulling her cloak tightly around her.

'Scared?'

She shook her head, her hand automatically lifting to her face. 'No, but where is the powder room?'

I pointed it out.

'Over there. Meet you at the bar, and don't take all night.'

She smiled briefly and I stood watching her as she crossed the foyer. I shook my head irritably. I didn't like the emotions I was feeling, and so I headed towards the bar. Two drinks later and I felt her nearness. Three drinks later and we began to talk.

Her name was Lorna, and she was an orphan, lived alone, was five years younger than me — and was an Anti.

She didn't tell me the last, but there are little tricks of conversation, verbal traps, subtle ways of finding out things, and I'd started with a healthy suspicion. I didn't tell her that I knew, I didn't tell her anything, that could come later, if at all, but now I was after a good time.

We had a few more drinks and some decent food. I lost a little cash at a dice game, and hesitated at the door of the happy-smoke lounge, looking at Lorna.

'Care for some sweet dreams?'

She shook her head, wrinkling her nose

with disgust and looking through the arched doorway I had to agree with her dislike.

Couches lined the walls and soft lights threw a mysterious haze over the furnishings of the room. It gave the place an exotic air, a romantic air, and it was as phony as hell. Men and women sprawled on the couches, looking like a collection of rag dolls with their limp limbs and slack staring faces. Soft-footed attendants moved between them carrying long-stemmed pipes and the odour of poppy poison hung thickly on the air.

I shrugged and moved away.

We drank a little and danced a lot, cheek to cheek stuff, though I could sense that she wasn't used to it, and had her mind more on her makeup than on me. I sat in at a poker game for an hour winning enough for the evening, then smiled at her as I steered her to a back room.

A ring stood in the centre of the room, seats circled it, and bright lights glared down from above. We took ringside seats and while waiting for the bout to commence I took the chance to scan the crowd.

Nothing.

No enemies, at least no known enemies. No black looks or frowns or whispers. I could relax and feel safe here and I was glad of it. I didn't feel in the mood for action.

The bout was between a middle-aged man and a lithe young girl. They fought naked with knives and the man was outclassed from the start. He tried, any man would try when his life depended on it, but he was outmatched from the beginning and the girl slashed him to ribbons within five minutes.

The next bout was a three-way battle — all men. It was fun to watch, and I marked one of the combatants down as a good fighter. He mixed brawn and brain, letting the other two engage and stepping in when he could strike without opposition. They fought bare handed, the anything-goes technique, and my man won without having to kill either of the other two.

Other bouts followed, all designed to

appeal to raw emotions, and the audience seemed to approve of the promoter's choice. I glanced at Lorna from time to time, and when it seemed that she was about to vomit, I decided that it was time to go.

She clung to me in the cab. I had expected the reaction and was ready for it, but somehow it wasn't what it should have been. The house-guard didn't look at me when we arrived home. The girl couldn't have upset him, so it must have been the extra work I'd given him, that and getting reprimanded for having allowed assassins to enter the building.

A man had the right to expect some sort of protection when he paid the rent I did.

I grinned at the man, enjoying his discomfiture.

'Any goons waiting for me this time?'

'No.' He seemed about to choke. 'I couldn't help that, Mr. Carter. They must have sneaked past me, or entered as guests of some other tenant.'

'Naturally,' I said coldly. 'That explains perfectly how they got into my apartment.' I held out my hand. 'Well, goodbye, I hope that you've another job lined up — you'll be needing it.'

'Mr. Carter.' Sweat glistened on his worried face and I could guess how he felt as he appealed to me. 'I couldn't help what happened, and I promise you it won't occur again. Will you speak for me?'

'Why?'

'If I get kicked out of this job I'm finished.' He grabbed at my arm, his eyes desperate. 'You know how it is, once a guard falls down on the job he's blacklisted all over the city. I've a wife, Mr. Carter, I've got a couple of kids!'

'I've only got one life,' I said coldly. It was in my mind to give it to him, but something stopped me. Irritably I shrugged off his hand.

'Forget it,' I snapped. 'But the next time will be the last.'

The elevator doors cut off his grateful babble.

They had cleaned the apartment and aside from a lighter patch on the carpet there was nothing to show what had happened there. I locked the door and switched on the lights, turning on the radio as I went to the kitchen for ice and drinks.

Lorna was still standing in the centre of the room, her cloak drawn tightly about her slender figure and her eyes wide and frightened looking. I set down the drinks and smiled at her.

'Relax, I'm not going to eat you.'

'I shouldn't have come here,' she whispered. 'I don't know what made me do it.'

'Relax,' I said again, and poured out a stiff drink. 'Here, this will make you feel better.'

She took it, more from politeness than anything else, but I could tell that she was all keyed up inside and it worried me. Girls didn't act like that nowadays, not girls of her age and position, and I'd known enough of them to be able to tell.

But — she was different.

I took her by the hands and led her to the big easy chair, forcing her into it and sitting on the wide arm.

'Lorna,' I said gently. 'You don't have to be afraid, you know. Don't you trust me?'

She stared at me with her wide eyes, and I could almost see my reflection in their pupils. A hard faced man with a knife-scarred cheek and a puffed broken nose. I'd lived hard in my time, eaten well when I could and starved when I couldn't. A life like that leaves its mark on a man, and I'd never been particularly handsome to start with.

'It isn't that,' she whispered. 'It isn't that at all, its . . . ' Automatically her hand went to her face, to her worn makeup and the mottled skin. I laughed.

'Is that what troubles you?' I took her hand between mine and stared directly into her eyes. 'Forget it.'

'I can't, Jim. I can't! You don't know, you can't know what it means to a girl.'

'Forget it,' I said harshly. 'The world is what it is and we must take what we can get.'

'Is that how you feel about it?' She rose to her feet, putting down her untouched drink. 'I should have known better but I was a fool. I thought . . . '

'What did you think?' I stepped before her, knowing that if she went now I would never see her again. It shouldn't have troubled me, but it did.

'Never mind.' She blinked, her eyes filling with unshed tears and almost I hated myself. Whatever else happened, whatever else I did one thing I had to do. I had to restore the trust between us. I had to!

It was easy, too easy. It was unfair, but I didn't care for fairness not now, and soon I had her smiling again. I held her in my arms, not too tightly, and felt the stir of unfamiliar emotions as I looked into her eyes and at her lips. I bent, and she pulled away.

'Lorna!'

'Wait.' She smiled at me, and I knew what the effort cost her. 'There is something you must see.'

'It doesn't matter. Believe me, Lorna it doesn't matter!'

'It does matter, Jim,' she said quietly. 'To me.'

The bathroom door closed softly behind her.

I stood waiting, looking at the untouched drinks and striding about the apartment. The bathroom door clicked, and slowly she entered the room. I stepped towards her, then stopped, my eyes searching her face.

She had washed off every trace of makeup, dispensed with every artificial aid, and what I saw no woman should ever have been cursed with.

She wasn't deformed, she wasn't ugly, she wasn't inhuman, but her skin was — different.

It was mottled, discoloured in a regular pattern, a tortoiseshell pattern of angry reds and blues, yellows and sickening white. A grotesque mask stared at me, a mask from which two eyes glistened with tears and the gleam of white teeth shone between carmine lips.

I stared at it. I stared at it — and .then past it. I moved, stepping towards her, folding her in my arms and her lips were warm and utterly human.

And I knew then what I hadn't known before.

* * *

Branscome called me next morning. He snarled at me from the screen, then, as he saw my puffed and swollen features, grinned.

'Trouble?'

'No. What did you call for?'

'How's the job?'

I shrugged. 'Moving, why?'

'Things have been happening. The guards of the laboratories are going to make a general sweep of the lower sector. A combination. If you've any ideas better get moving, we haven't much time.'

'What do you expect?' I couldn't help sounding bitter. 'Miracles? A paper gets stolen from a guarded building. It could be anywhere in the city and you expect me to get it back within hours.'

'You've done it before.'

'That was different. I can track stolen goods, but this isn't the same.'

'Perhaps not, but if you hope to get paid for what you've done you'll find it.' He leered at me. 'How's the girl?'

I didn't answer, just stood staring at the flickering surface of the screen. Branscome had probably learned about her from one of his touts, maybe from the beggars or even the house-guard, but I didn't like the idea of his spying on me.

He licked his lips, running a grimy finger against the side of his nose, and for some reason I began to hate his pasty face.

'You know about her?'

'I know,' I said curtly, and cut the connection. I was annoyed to find that my hands were trembling, and angrily swallowed a drink. Damn Branscome! Damn the missing papers! Damn the whole unholy mess!

I tilted the bottle again.

It was still cold and though it had stopped snowing, big white drifts stood piled against the sides of the buildings. I stood on the edge of the sidewalk, my breath coming in thick plumes and felt the cold begin to bite into me. I wanted hot coffee. I wanted to rest at a table and watch Lorna as she moved with her long-legged easy grace. I wanted to do a lot of things, but I had to get on with the job.

I walked. Partly to keep warm but

mostly because where I was going a cab would be as out of place as a diamond necklace around a beggar's neck. I strode along the ice-covered pavement ignoring the frozen bodies of those who had died during the night and trying not to see the pitiful gestures of the homeless. It was bad but it couldn't be helped.

The residential section gave way to the business and shopping centres. I passed the markets, diving down little alleys and heading for the old waterfront. Traffic had almost vanished from the streets and pedestrians were few and far between. Half-a-mile more and I was where I had wanted to be.

A smell hung over the place. An odour, half-rot, half-musk. It coiled between the sagging bulks of warehouses and rose from the gutters. It reeked of dirt and unwashed bodies, of bad cooking and festering sores. It was a familiar smell, too familiar.

The smell of poverty.

I paused by a low doorway, knocking in a series of swift raps using the heavy signet ring on my right hand. A judas grill opened and little eyes stared at me from the darkness within. A pause then chains rattled and the door swung open.

A man stood and grinned at me. A twisted caricature of what a man should be. A scar plucked at his lips and one shoulder rose higher than the other. He moved, and his trailing foot left a thin line in the dust.

'Jim! Anything wrong?'

'No.' I ducked through the door and waited as the bolts and chains rattled back home. He jerked his head at me and moved towards the rear of the building, moving like a broken-backed spider as he trailed his useless limb. I followed him, one hand resting on the gun beneath my jacket. I should be safe here, but gratitude can be a funny thing.

A dim bulb shone a sickly light over a rough table and the remains of some noisome meal rested among the ruins of several bottles.

The cripple swept them away, clearing a space at the end of the table, and I sat on an upturned box.

'Haven't seen you for a long time, Jim.'

The cripple fumbled beneath a heap of rags and lifted a dirty bottle. 'How are things with you?'

'Not so good.' I watched as he poured two cracked mugs full of a thick red wine. I sipped at the stuff, almost gagged, then forced myself to empty the mug. He grinned, and tilted the bottle, refilling my container.

'Just like old times, eh, Jim. Remember the old days? Before I fell off a roof and you had to drag me to the hospital for treatment.' He sighed, staring at his wine. 'Great days, Jim. Great days. We made a good team.'

'We could again,' I said, and tried to ignore the prickling between my shoulder blades. He shook his head.

'No, Jim. Those days are over. If it hadn't been for you I'd have died from that fall, and sometimes I wish that I had.' He glared at me, little flecks of foam appearing at the comers of his mouth.

Suddenly I knew that someone had entered the room.

I didn't move. I didn't even breathe. I was a stranger here, a stranger wearing clothes worth the price of a month's food, a week's drug supply, a night at one of the happy-smoke joints. I sat as if made of stone, my brain whirling inside my head, and a thin film of sweat starting over my face.

The cripple laughed.

'Relax,' he said, and gestured to someone standing behind me. 'Beat it, Jim here is a friend of mine, and don't you forget it.'

Air drifted about me, a thin stream of clean coldness, then the prickling between my shoulders died, and I could breathe again.

'What can I do for you, Jim?'

'I'm looking for a paper, Max,' I said gently. 'It was stolen from the laboratories of Atomic Power Inc., a bit of stiff blue paper covered with scribble. They want it back.'

'Do they?' He smiled and reached for the bottle. 'Worth much?'

'Five thousand.'

He sat in thought, twirling the half-empty bottle between his hands. He looked at me, and I tried to read his dull black eyes, I failed.

'I haven't got it,' he said. 'None of my boys could have got it. Atomic Power you say?'

'Yes.'

Silence. Silence as we each sat busy with our own secret thoughts. Carefully I picked up the thick mug.

'Any ideas?'

He shrugged, the gesture grotesque and somehow horrible, and then sat biting at his flabby lips.

'Tried the Antis?'

'No. Should I?'

He laughed, a thick gurgling laughter without mirth and without any real feeling except that of hate. Abruptly the bottle shattered beneath his grip and he sat staring stupidly at the blood staining his hand.

'Why not?' he said thickly. 'They go for that sort of stuff, don't they? Atomics! Bombs! Everything like that. They want to rule us, don't they? Tell us what to do, how to do it and God help us if we don't. Antis! Swine!'

'Where can I contact them?'

'You ask me that!' He rose from the table and stood glaring down at me, rage twisting his features. 'Get out! Get out before I forget that we once were friends! Get out now!'

I didn't argue. I never argue with maniacs, children — or old friends. I rose to my feet, not saying anything, not looking anything, not even thinking anything. All I wanted was to get out alive.

He unchained the door, jerking it open and letting in a gust of freezing wind. I stepped through it, then turned and stared at the distorted face of the cripple.

'Max,' I said urgently. 'Max!'

'Get away from me,' he said, and his voice sounded almost like a sob. 'Anti lover!'

I stared at the slammed door, wishing that we hadn't parted as we had, tasting the bad taste of defeat, and regretting the past. It did no good, the door remained shut and I turned away.

Half-a-mile down the street a beggar bumped into me. He hit my arm, the bad one, and I felt sick at the sudden wash of pain. A second rose up at my side, grabbing my arm, and a third swung something at my head.

I kicked, feeling bone snap and hearing a scream of agony. I smashed my hand into a dirty face, the heavy signet ring laying open his cheek to the bone. I twisted, jerking at the retaining arm, then something smashed down onto my head.

The stiffened nylon of my cap took the full force of the blow saving me from a splintered skull, but I went down on my knees. They hit me again, and the star-shot blackness of oblivion roared about me. Someone kicked me and someone else hissed a sharp word of warning.

Then the pavement opened beneath me and I was falling, falling, falling.

Falling into a black eternity.

* * *

It was cold. It was cold with the deathly chill of deep blue ice, of frozen air, of the vast distances between the stars. It was too cold for any living thing, too cold for ghosts, too cold for even the fierce heat of the atom. It was too cold to be stood any longer.

I groaned, rolling over on my side, and the dull ache of my injured arm jerked me to pain-shot awareness. I shivered, my teeth chattering as I felt the bite of the icy wind and the burning cold of the frozen snow beneath me.

Painfully I sat upright, nursing my swollen head between hands that felt like blocks of wood, trying to still the churning of my stomach.

I fumbled at my clothing searching for cigarettes, then glanced down when I couldn't find my pockets. My clothing was gone! I wore rags, thin and dirty, torn and tattered, they flapped in the bitter wind and I could see naked flesh through great rents in the rotten material. My rings were gone, my gun, my money. I staggered to my feet and felt snow against my bare soles. I felt sick and numb with desperation and the after-effects of the beating up.

The worst was yet to come.

I saw it by the weak light of an overhead fluorescent reflected from the steel shutters of a closed shop. A streak across my forehead, a red streak, oddly shaped and unmistakable.

The debtor's brand!

Even then I didn't worry too much. I had been robbed, beaten, branded, but I still had a home, a bank account and a few friends.

Painfully I staggered along the sidewalk heading back into the heart of the city.

It was dark and I must have been unconscious for most of the day, but I couldn't have been lying in the frozen snow for that length of time. A sour taste in my mouth gave the answer. I had been dragged to some form of shelter, drugged, and then thrown out when it was time for me to recover. I frowned as I thought of it, beggars wouldn't have done that, they wouldn't have cared if I lived or died, but then beggars wouldn't have beaten me up in the first place.

Lights blazed above the entrance to my apartment house and I leaned wearily against the bell. I needed a bath, fresh clothes, a slug of liquor and a good night's sleep.

I didn't get either.

A grill slammed open and a harsh voice echoed across the deserted street.

'What do you want?'

'What do you think?' I snapped tiredly. My head had begun to ache and what with that and the pain from my arm I was in no mood to bandy words. 'Let me in, I live here.'

'You what?'

'Hell, man, let me in!' I stared at him, and received another shock. I didn't know the house-guard, he was unfamiliar to me, and I could guess what he was thinking.

'Look,' I said urgently. 'I live here, room three sixty, Carter, Jim Carter. I've been robbed and beaten up. Let me in.'

'Sure,' he said sarcastically. 'I'll let you in — as soon as you show me your house-identification.'

'Don't be a fool! I told you that I've been robbed.' I stared impatiently at him. 'Where's the other guard?'

'Canned.' He stepped back from the

grill. 'Sorry, but you don't get in, take it up with the office in the morning.' The judas door slammed on my protests.

I couldn't blame him, he was paid to guard the building and residents, and with jobs as scarce as they were he wasn't taking any chances. I turned from the door, rubbing my hand over my forehead, then stared down at the traces of red on my fingers.

I should have known.

Tattooing would have left my forehead a throbbing sore, and the debtor's mark was always tattooed. Someone had smeared a red stain over my forehead, smeared it on after beating me up and stealing my clothes. They had done it for a reason. I began to wonder why.

Wind lashed at me, numbing my exposed flesh and jerking me to full awareness of my position. Tomorrow I could enter the apartment, my thumb-print was on record and they would let me in. Tomorrow I could draw money from the bank, get new clothes and weapons, wash off the red brand, but that was tomorrow.

Unless I found shelter soon I wouldn't be alive tomorrow, I would join the beggars frozen in the night or be shot down by some guard with a suspicious nature. I had to get shelter and that meant that I had to get money.

It wasn't easy.

I hung around outside a happy-smoke joint, thrusting my way forward, jerking the opposition from my path, and stuck my hand before each and every couple entering or leaving the joint. I chose a couple because there was less chance of getting my hand knocked off, and just when I had about given up hope I got what I was after.

A blonde, skillfully dressed, professionally bored, languidly beautiful, stumbled as I tripped her, then watched approvingly as I knocked down some poor devil at my side, blaming him for what he hadn't done.

I pulled my punch as much as I dared, and would even have shared my reward had it been larger. I felt that bad.

But I was fixed for the night.

* * *

The doss-house was a rambling warehouse deep in the poorer part of town. A great rambling structure with blind shuttered windows, sagging walls, and a single barred door. A man sat just within the entrance, a big man ugly with fat and wearing a holstered pistol strapped round his bulging paunch. He stared at me, swinging a club, and making little slobbering noises with his flabby lips.

'Whatcha want?'

'A flop in the warm.' I showed him my money. 'Any objections?' He spat and held out his hand, examining the coin.

'Hungry?'

I nodded and he tucked the coin in his pocket. 'Grab some chow inside, one bowl. Any noise and you're out.' He jerked his head and I entered the interior of the warehouse.

It stank.

It reeked of dirt and stale food, of sweat and vermin, of too many bodies in too small an area. I felt saliva pour into my mouth as the smell hit me in the face, and hesitated, trying not to breathe, A blast of icy wind from the closing door helped make up my mind, and I went on in.

The chow was a single bowl of greasy slop. It reeked of sour yeast and bad soy, of reclaimed garbage and the scrapings of a thousand dirty plates, but it was warm, edible, and I forced myself to gulp it down.

Dim bulbs threw a vague light over the interior and I could see rows of silent shapes each muffled in their rags and pressing close to each other for warmth. A woman stared at me as I walked along looking for an empty place, a thin faced woman with lank dirty hair and wild dark eyes. She simpered at me, then as she saw the brand on my forehead, cursed and covered her face.

I took no notice.

The floor was hard and cold, but not as cold as the pavement outside. I stretched, trying to ease the ache in my bones and feeling the alternate sweat and chill of incipient fever. Tomorrow I would have to get some prophylactic shots. Tomorrow I would have to get anti-flu and anti-pneumonia injections. Tomorrow. Tomorrow. Always tomorrow.

Things began to take on an unreal appearance. The silent rows of muffled shapes looked like corpses, the warehouse a giant mortuary lit by the dying stars of vanishing hope. Or perhaps it was the anteroom to hell and we were lost souls waiting for the fires of purgatory.

Lost souls. Scum washed on the shores of a disintegrating civilisation. The damned!

Someone moaned softly from the other side of the room, and someone else cursed in a low savage monotone. The big man strode between the silent rows, his club swinging from his hand. A sharp crack and the moaning stopped. He was grinning as he returned.

I shifted a little, and the man next to me grunted, turning in his sleep, and uncovering his face. I stared at it, at the thick growth of stubble, the shape of the ears and neck — and at the vivid red streak across his forehead.

I had seen that face before.

I had seen it on a scrap of paper, a photograph caught by the spy camera and

I tensed as he mumbled and opened his eyes.

We stared at each other, and I could sense his quick suspicion, his guarded distrust, then as he saw my own brand, quick relief. He licked his lips and nodded.

'Is it morning yet?'

'No.'

He sighed, and rolled over on his side trying for sleep. I knew he couldn't and lay waiting for him to talk. He did, keeping his voice low and shooting suspicious looks around him as he whispered in the heavy reek.

'A hell of a night.' He paused, rubbing automatically at his forehead. 'I see you've got one too, how?'

'The usual,' I forced bitterness into my tones, 'a debt, a lousy fifty and they wouldn't give me time to pay.'

He nodded sympathetically. 'I know. I owed a little more than that, two hundred, but they clamped down on me without warning.' He twisted his lips, hate distorting his grimed features.

'The dirty swine! With all that they've

got they had to clamp down.'

'Atomic Power Inc.?'

He looked at me with quick suspicion, his eyes guarded and I could sense his regret at having said too much. I smiled.

'They got me too, they get everyone, and they always operate the same way. Pay up — or else!'

'Yeah.' He stared past me into the dim distance and licked his lips as if at a pleasant thought. 'It's time someone paid them off for what they've done.'

'How?' I rolled on my back and pretended disinterest. 'What can a man do against them? They've got too many guards too many high walls, too much protection. What can one man do?'

'Plenty.' He trembled on the brink of telling me what I wanted to know, and I smiled into the dimness. He had bottled it up too long, he had to tell, to boast, to spill his guts and bask in stolen glory. Wasn't I his friend? Didn't I also wear the brand of the damned? Wasn't I safe?

Iron footsteps rang on the stained concrete and the lights blazed to an eye-searing brilliance.

They came with stabbing handbeams, ready weapons and swinging clubs. They came with mechanical precision, deploying with the smooth efficiency of long training and their faces were hard and stern beneath the peaked visors of their uniform caps

The guards of Atomic Products Inc.

I had forgotten them, forgotten all about the big combined operation to sweep the lower section of the town. I watched them as they jabbed sleeping men into wakefulness and stared stonily at the twisted faces of cursing women. They blocked the door and with quick blows of their clubs they forced obedience from the muttering crowd.

Then they began to search every man and woman in the place.

I heard the man at my side curse with a desperate intensity. He half-lunged to his feet, then fell back with a sob as he realised that escape was impossible. I clutched at his arm.

'You got matches?'

'What?' His eyes were wild and I had to repeat my question before he understood.

‘Sure. Why?’

‘Give them to me. Quick!’

The floor wouldn’t burn, but the walls were of rotten wood and should flare well. I slipped the matches in my pocket and sauntered towards the guards. They stared at me and silently I began to undress, submitting quietly to their search, then stepping to one side as I dressed again.

A can of oil for the heater beneath the cook pot stood by the door. I jerked out the stopper, splashed it over the wall, and before they knew what I intended, had struck a match and thrown it at the fluid.

A sheet of flame raced up the woodwork.

It was beautiful, a red curtain of flames burning away all the dirt and all the rottenness of the lice-ridden doss-house, sending little sparks flying in the breeze from the half-open door and starting a dozen other fires. A woman screamed, the shrill sound slashing across the crackle of flame and the startled cursing of the guards. One of them snarled at me, raising his pistol and squeezing the trigger. I ducked, the high-velocity bullet screaming over my head. The next moment all hell broke loose.

The place was a death trap with only one exit, the door! The guards didn't stand a chance, they went down cursing and shooting uselessly at the stampeding crowd. Blood rilled from where they had dropped, red blood staining the soiled concrete, staining bare feet and dirty rags. Blood from lives stamped out on hard cement. I slipped through the door and stood against the side of the building.

Waiting.

I didn't have to wait long.

He came, red-eyed and weeping from smoke and fear, coughing and beating at his smouldering rags, the brand on his forehead bright and clear in the light from the burning building. He stood trembling with reaction and the terror of near death, then walked unsteadily towards the edge of town.

I followed him.

I followed him past silent buildings, looming high and dim towards the dark sky. I followed him along narrow alleys and over heaped debris covered with snow. I followed him until my feet were numb and my arm throbbed with a shrieking agony, until the wind no longer seared my naked flesh with cold and my hand felt as if made of wood.

Then he stopped, and I sat beside him.

He wasn't too surprised. He stared at me, his stubbled face thin and drawn and his eyes dull with defeat.

'I knew that you were after me,' he said. 'What do you want?'

'The paper.' I didn't waste words. 'The paper you stole from the laboratories of Atomic Power Inc. Give.'

'I haven't got it,' he lied weakly, not really expecting to be believed. 'I passed it on.'

I swung at his jaw, using my right hand and putting the muscles of back and shoulder to work. He grunted once before keeling over and before he had fallen my hands were roving over his body.

I found it in a body belt, a thin wad of stiff blue paper nestling in a double fold of the nylon. I took it and rose wearily to my feet, staring down at the slumped figure before me.

There was nothing I could do for him. Nothing.

Painfully I stumbled through the snow.

Dawn found me half-dead with cold waiting outside the apartment building. They were suspicious, and I couldn't blame them but they had changed the guard to a man I knew, and after some argument they checked my thumbprint and let me in.

The shower felt wonderful, the hot coffee even better and it was good to have clean clothes on my back again. I'd scrubbed off the red stain and checked the loading of my spare gun. I swallowed some pills to clear up the incipient fever then called Branscome on the videophone.

He didn't answer.

I made three other calls and then managed to contact Lorna. I smiled at her, noting her wide-eyed look of surprise.

'Hello, darling. When do I see you?'

'You want to?' She bit her lip and I noticed that she had taken trouble with her makeup.

'What do you think?' I became serious. 'Of course I want to see you, can you come right over?'

She nodded, and I stood for a long while staring at the blank screen. Then I rang down to the house-guard telling him to admit her, and tried to get Branscome again.

Same result.

I took a drink, then another, and after a while a third. I felt restless and stood at the window staring down at the city. The wind was from the mainland and I could guess the hell brewing below. There would be fighting and short tempers, emotional disturbances and a craving for euphoria. The happy-smoke joints would be busy — and so would the dead-wagons.

A nice town.

The dark figures of beggars sprawled on the pavements, ruined debris of humanity lost in the canyons between locked and guarded havens of refuge. The weak, the handicapped, the lost souls clinging to obsolete conventions and being trampled by the iron feet of progress.

I took another drink.

The doorbell chimed and Lorna entered the room. I stepped towards her, feeling her presence ease my restlessness and wishing that she need never go. We stared at each other for a moment, then I gestured with my glass, she nodded and I poured a generous measure.

'Here's to us.' I smiled at her, then drank, feeling the bite of the alcohol as it went down my throat.

'Why did you send for me, Jim?'

'I wanted to talk with you, that's one reason.'

'Is there another?' She sipped at her drink then set it down on the table. I took her shoulders in my hands and stared into her eyes.

'Yes,' I said. 'Do you want to hear it?'

'I don't know.' She twisted from my grip, her hand going automatically to her face. 'Jim, that night, you mustn't think . . . '

'I learned all I need to know that night, and you needn't worry.'

'You know?'

'Yes, but it doesn't matter, Lorna. It doesn't matter!'

'You said that once before, Jim. I want to believe you, but how can I? You've seen me, seen all of me, how can any man love a thing like that?'

'Stop it!' I shouted angrily. 'Stop it I say!'

My hands were trembling and I slopped some of my drink on the table as I tilted the bottle. I couldn't look at her, I daren't, I couldn't trust myself. 'I told you that it didn't matter, isn't that good enough?'

'You know what I am, Jim,' she said quietly. 'You know that, don't you?'

'What of it?' I forced myself to face her. 'What difference does it make? I love you. I love you no matter what you are. Can't you leave it at that?'

'I wish I could, I wish to God I could!' She smiled at me through her tears, not worrying about her ruined makeup. 'I love you too, Jim. Love you as I never thought that I'd ever be able to love a man, but it's no good, Jim. It's no good!'

'Why not?'

'Because I'm a mutant, Jim, that's why. A mutant! Now do you see?'

'No.' I stepped close to her, staring into her face. 'It doesn't matter, not one little bit.' I nodded at the startled comprehension in her eyes.

'You see — I'm the same as you.'

'You mean?'

I nodded, feeling unutterably relieved.

We sat on the edge of the couch our forgotten drinks on the table, holding hands as if we were kids just out of school. She had cried a little, whether they were tears of joy or sadness I didn't know, but one thing was certain.

We didn't intend to part.

She smiled up at me, dabbing at her ruined makeup and squeezed my hand.

'What else did you want to see me about, Jim?'

I sighed, wishing that life could stop just as it was, but it had to be said.

'What made you become an Anti, Lorna?'

I felt her stiffen. I sensed her startled reaction, her half-fear, half-shame that I knew, but she had courage and I didn't have to repeat the question.

'What else could I become, Jim? Life isn't easy for the weak, look at the beggars, look at the debtors, look at the drug-crazed children and the dead in the streets every morning. We want to stop all that, Jim. We want law and order, a decent life and protection for the weak. Is that wrong?'

I didn't answer, but drew her to the window and pointed to the edge of town.

'Look at those ruins,' I said, and my voice didn't seem to be my own. 'Look beyond them, at the deadlands and the radioactive hell around us. Law and order did that. Protecting the weak and defending the helpless. They had police in the old days, and arms and weapons to be used by armies. What danger is one man? He can shoot and kill — but he can be killed in turn.'

I shook my head.

'I want freedom, Lorna. Freedom in the truest sense of the word. My gun, my arms against the guns and arms of those who want to 'protect' me. I want freedom, the power to hit at those who hurt me. With your law and order I couldn't have that. I'd have to go whining to police or armies, and what could they do?'

'They could help us, Jim. They would stop crime.'

'Crime?' I laughed contemptuously. 'What is crime? There is none. Without law and law enforcement how can there be crime?'

I drew her to me and tasted the sweetness of her lips.

It was a funny world. I thought of Branscome and his allergy to water so that washing to him was a thing too painful to be borne. I thought of the crippled body and twisted mind of an old friend. I thought of my mother, now dead, and of my father still living. I thought of the difference between me and other men, of the knack I had of reading minds when their natural barriers were relaxed at moments of emotional stress.

I thought of a lot of things.

The click of the door jerked me back to sense, and I spun, my hand grabbing at the butt of my pistol. Branscome stood just within the room, his dirt-streaked face wearing a loose smile and his hands empty.

'Busy, Jim?'

'I might be.' I looked at him. 'I tried to contact you, but you wouldn't answer. Why not?'

He shrugged, slamming the door behind him, and helping himself to my liquor. I made a mental note to see that the house-guard got canned. He had no right letting anyone into the building without warning.

'I was visiting a friend,' he said calmly, 'then I decided to drop in.' He held out his hand. 'Give it to me.'

I stared at him.

'Give you what?'

'The papers.' He made a little rubbing motion with his thumb and forefinger. 'Give.'

'I haven't got them.'

He sighed, tilting my bottle and looking at me from beneath untidy eyebrows. 'Don't lie, Jim. Not to me. I know you have them, you got them last night after the fire. They're useless to you, but I want them.'

I shook my head, smiling into his face and moving so as to keep Lorna out of the line of fire.

'Don't be a fool, Jim! What good are they to you?'

I shrugged. 'Twenty thousand?'

'I'll give you ten, you'd never get more. Well?'

'No.'

He tightened his lips, little sparks of anger flashing in his dull eyes. 'Jim,' he said carefully. 'I'll give you one more chance. You should know by now what I can do. Either you give me those papers — or next time the brand won't wash off.'

I stood looking down at him, at his straggling hair and dirt stained neck. I had known it. I knew him too well to be fooled and I could read him like an open book. I knew what he wanted.

Power.

He wasn't alone in that. There had always been men like him and there always would be. Potential dictators, greedy for what they wanted and not caring how they got it. Usually they didn't last long. Usually they trod on one set of toes too many and knife or gun settled the score. It was the best way.

He stared into my eyes and what he

saw there made him tremble in sudden fear.

'Jim,' he whispered. 'Don't look at me like that. I wouldn't harm you, you know that. I'm your friend, your best friend. Jim!'

'You had the beggars in your pay,' I said grimly. 'You had an arrangement with Max and played along with the Antis at the same time. You knew too much about Lorna, and you had me beaten up. Why, Branscome? Why?'

I didn't need to ask the question, but I wanted him to damn himself from his own mouth. Killing him would come easier then.

'They crossed me,' he whined. 'I bought a plan of the laboratories, bribed the guards, hired the men. They got what I wanted, and then they crossed me. I knew you could find the papers and I sent you to where I knew they must be.' He licked his flabby lips. 'It was the only way, Jim. I was fighting against time and I had to find the papers. I had to!'

'Why?'

Lorna crossed the room and stood

before me staring down at the fear-crazed man. I tried to push her to one side, afraid lest Branscome should pull a gun, but she smiled at me and shook her head.

'What are those papers? Why are they so important to you?'

'To us, Lorna,' he whispered. 'To us.' He swallowed and glanced furtively at me. 'They hold the secret of controlled atomic fission and with them we could remake the bomb. Once we have that then we can force law and order on this chaos, break the big cartels and give the Antis a chance to take over. We could clean up the city, wipe out the mutants, force the farmers to send us food. It would mean a fresh start, Lorna. A strong man could gain full control and enforce his own peace.'

'And you would be the strong man.'

I pushed Lorna to one side and this time she didn't resist me. Branscome looked at me, then at her, then down at the clean spot on the carpet.

'Why not?'

I didn't answer him. I wanted to kill him, to blast him where he sat and end the danger of him getting his own way forever, but it would have done no good. He wasn't the only one, and it seemed hard to kill a man for his dreams.

And then there was Lorna.

I stared at my trembling hands, feeling the bite of wind-borne atoms from the radioactive deadlands as their radiation disturbed delicate neuron paths. At such times violence came too easily.

'Get out!'

He looked at me, not moving.

'Get out before I blast you. Get out and never let me see you again. Get out, now!'

He swallowed, not able to credit his luck, then as awareness came he scuttled towards the door. I stood fighting the hate within me as I heard him go.

'Thank you.' Lorna stood before me and smiled into my face

'You heard him,' I said thickly. 'You heard what he said. Wipe out the mutants, rule beneath the threat of the bomb. Kill you, me, my father, kill all the poor devils who couldn't help being born.'

'You let him go.'

'Yes, I let him go.'

I stared at her, trying to find in her features the reason for my action. She put her arms around me.

'Thank you,' she repeated, and kissed me full on the lips.

I clung to her, pressing her close to me and feeling my hate dissolving. I kissed her hair, her cheeks, her throat and the soft fullness of her lips.

I didn't even hear the click of the lock.

They stood just within the open door, three of them, armed, uniformed in solemn black, their eyes hard and watchful beneath the peaked visors of their helmets. They stared about the room, one of them searching the bathroom and one the kitchen, the other standing by the door.

Watching.

Satisfied, they took up their positions, standing against the walls their hands resting on the uncovered butts of their pistols. It wasn't until then that the fourth man entered the room.

He was old, white-haired and with skin wrinkled like the peel of an over-stored apple. He looked at me with shrewd little eyes, bobbed politely to Lorna, and sat carefully in the easy chair.

'Shall we get down to business?' His voice was a thin squeak rasping from a too-tight throat, but I didn't laugh.

'You have it?'

He nodded, fumbling in his pocket and producing a printed slip of paper. 'Twenty thousand, the sum agreed on. Will you accept a cheque?'

I nodded. There were few people or organisations that I'd trust for an unverified cheque, but Atomic Power Inc. was one of them. They were big.

'Very well, now the papers, please.' He held out a hand thin and wasted and looking like the claw of some giant bird. I pulled the thin wad of papers from my pocket and dropped them into his palm. He sat jiggling them for a moment, looking at me with his shrewd eyes.

'Have you looked at these?'

'No.'

'Could copies have been made, photocopies?'

'No.'

'You are sure of that? Quite sure?'

I laughed curtly and shrugged. 'You should know. Haven't your guards covered every photographer in town, every place where copies could be made? Wouldn't your advertised reward have smoked them out if they had? They haven't been copied, you can take my word for it.'

He nodded as if satisfied, then thrust the papers into his pocket

'You know what they are?'

'Yes. A man told me, the man who arranged for them to be stolen.' I shook my head at his unspoken question. 'No, he didn't look at them, he never had them, his thief crossed him up.'

'Are you sure?'

I sighed, and deliberately poured a drink. Lorna didn't say a word, just stood staring at the silent guards, her features tense and worried.

'Yes, I'm sure.' I swallowed the liquor. 'He made a mistake, a small one but it proved fatal. He gave me a photograph taken by a spy camera. A photograph taken at night and it showed a man's face.'

He nodded with quiet understanding.

'I see. The wind was from the mainland that night, the radiations would have ruined the film.'

'Not only that. If the photograph had been genuine there would have been no need to call in outside agencies. I checked, and no such aid had been asked. He was getting desperate and had to take a chance. He montaged the photograph to show the face of his thief and then set me on the trail. He never even saw what he had paid for.'

He smiled and pushed the cheque towards me, then tapped at the pocket containing the papers.

'These are better with us. Unfortunately we can't have cheap plentiful power without also knowing how to make the bomb but we have learned our lesson. There will be no second atomic war.' He rose and held out his thin hand. 'Thank you, Mr. Carter. If you ever need employment let me know. I could use a man like you among my guards.'

I grinned and glanced at Lorna.

'Thank you, but I have other plans.'

'I suspected it, but bear my offer in mind.' He paused by the door while his guards searched the passage.

'Don't worry about your ex-employer. He will be taken care of, my guards will see to that. We can't have such a man threatening our freedom.'

He smiled again, bobbed his head at Lorna, and passed from the room.

And passed from my life.

* * *

The wind has risen, wailing against the high buildings and rattling the windows. I moved restlessly about the room, drinking a little, smoking a lot, and turning over a dozen plans for our future life.

We would be married, of course. It wasn't necessary, but some of the old conventions still had an appeal and I wanted to make Lorna mine for as long as we both should live. I would take a larger apartment, buy new furniture, hire a permanent guard and move into higher circles. I could do it, I had done it before, rising from the gutters and climbing to relative wealth and a life of ease.

I could climb higher. A determined man could do anything, and I was a determined man.

I told her of my plans, snapping quick sentences at her as she sat in the easy chair, and trying not to feel the irritation plucking at my brain. She smiled at me, then rose and stretched.

'If I'm to move in with you, dear, I'd better get my things.'

'I'll come with you,' I decided. 'We can be married on the way back and start as we intend to continue.' I helped her on with her cloak, automatically checking the loading of my gun.

'We'll have children, lots of them, not all mutants are sterile and I like kids. We can buy a small house, a protected one, of course, and I'll make enough to keep us both in luxury. Branscome was wrong, but he had some good ideas and I can improve on them.'

I babbled on like a kid with his first girlfriend, the words streaming from between my lips like bubbles from a foam-bath. She didn't say anything, just smiled at me with understanding eyes.

The house-guard saluted me as we came from the lift, he didn't say anything, but I knew that he was impressed by my visitors.

They had probably tipped him well.

Outside it was still cold. The tingling wind was bitter and the sullen clouds were loaded with snow. I stood on the edge of the pavement looking for a fleet cab, ignoring the pitiful wailing of the beggars sheltering against the wall.

I was careless.

I heard the whine of tyres, the purr of a turbine and displaced air lashed at me. A hand jerked me back, something warm and soft thrust at me and metal tore my sleeve.

I fell, slipping on the ice-covered sidewalk and cracking my elbow on the concrete. Something wet and sticky sprayed over me, something red and warm.

Blood.

I jerked to my feet, the gun leaping in my hand as I pumped shots after the speeding car. I was lucky. A rear tyre went out with a dull explosion and the car skidded helplessly, metal crunching as it slammed against a wall. A man staggered from the driving seat, a man with a dirt-streaked, pasty white face, long straggling hair and a loose screaming mouth.

Branscome.

I shot him. I smashed his arms, his legs, ripping his body with high-velocity bullets and spilling his guts in a red stream over the sidewalk. I cursed as I fired, snarling down at him without regret or remorse, hating myself for not doing before what I did now.

He was dead. With all his high dreams and greed for power, he was dead. He was just like any other dead man, like the frozen beggars, the knifed thieves, the stoned mutants. Dead. And like them he would wind up as fertiliser.

I wished him in hell.

I looked at Lorna then, staring down at her broken body, trying not to see where the blood had washed off her makeup. She was dead, of course. I had known that from the start. She had died to save me, thrusting her own body in front of the speeding car, and it was her blood that had splashed me.

I looked at her, feeling all my hopes and plans, all my dreams and happiness melt away at the touch of stern reality.

She was dead.

And looking down at her all my own words came like a thousand-footed army — and kicked me straight in the teeth.

My arms and gun against those of others who hurt me. Freedom to live as I wished, without restriction or restraint. Liberty to shoot and smash, to burn and destroy without regard for any other living soul.

Freedom!

I picked her up, holding her gently in my arms and not worrying about the blood ruining my clothes. I stared at her still, cold face, at the lips once so warm and the figure once so beautiful.

'Yeah,' I said, and didn't recognise the sound of my own voice. 'Freedom — it's wonderful!'

Softly I kissed the dead lips.

2

The Pensioners

There was something disquieting about the new neighbours. It wasn't just that they didn't own a car, though that in itself made them unique on Maple Avenue, but, as Martha Prentice emphasised, they didn't even have television.

'You can't be sure of that,' protested George. He was a chubby, over-fed, under-exercised man with a highly developed imagination and a firm set of prejudices. The imagination helped him to sell insurance. The prejudices were responsible for his looking ten years older than his actual middle-age. He reached out and buttered more toast.

'I am sure,' snapped Martha. Like her husband she was no longer young and was that type of woman who seem to become pickled with age. Her mouth looked like a prune and even her smile was vinegary. 'I watched them unload the van and there was no television. Besides,' she said triumphantly, 'if they had a set then where's the aerial?'

'Could be an indoor one.' George ate the last of his toast and helped himself to coffee. 'And what's so wrong in not owning a car? There's still a lot of people who don't own them.'

'Not on Maple Avenue, there aren't. Even if they were nervous of driving they could use one of the robot models like I do. No, George, there's something funny about them.' She meant peculiar, not amusing, but as George knew that she never found anything amusing he didn't make the mistake of assuming that she meant what she said. He sighed and glanced at his wristwatch.

'I don't like it,' said Martha, but from the expression in her eyes it was obvious that she did. 'For all we know they could be spies or criminals or something. You've got to do something about it, George.'

'Me?' He blinked, even for Martha this was something new. 'What can I do?'

'You can find out about them, that's what. I'll do my share and I want you to do yours. I haven't lived here for twenty years without having a right to know who and what my neighbours are.'

She darted to the window as footsteps crunched on the gravelled sidewalk running along the avenue. For a moment she tensed then, as the footsteps continued past the house and the one next door, she relaxed.

'And that's another thing. They never come out. I've only seen them once, when they first arrived, and that was a month ago.'

'Who was that?'

'Mr. Jorson, he lives five houses down. His wife's expecting again and they've had the doctor in three times during the past week.' She rattled off the information as though she were an information machine and he had pressed the right button. Talking of the Jorsons seemed to remind her of something for she patted her frizzy, greying hair and brushed the front of her dress. 'I think I'll just pop along and see if there's anything I can do.'

She stared hard at George. 'Don't forget now, find out all you can.'

He sighed again, but this time it was a sigh of defeat.

* * *

Their name was Randall and there were just the two of them. Both were fairly old and had arrived from a distant town. George gleaned that information from Fred Burns who had rented them the house and felt he owed it to the man to make some sort of explanation. They had known each other long enough for the explanation to be the true one.

'It's Martha,' he said. 'You know how women are. They get a bee in their bonnet and there's no shifting it.'

'I know how it is.' Fred nodded and looked sympathetic. 'Well, George that's all I can tell you. The whole transaction was done by mail and, to speak the truth, I've only seen them the once, that was when I handed them the keys.'

'Thanks anyway.' George hesitated. 'How do they pay?'

'By cheque on the Union Bank.'

'Regular?'

'Bankers order. No trouble there, George.' Fred seemed a little restless. 'Tell Martha to quit worrying. They're just a harmless couple wanting somewhere to settle down and die.'

George nodded. He knew that he had got all the information he could from the estate agent and, with the skill of long practice, changed the subject.

'Thanks again, Fred. How about you and Susan dropping over one night for a session? Martha'll do the cooking and I could ask a few of the boys over to make it a real party.'

'Martha's cooking!' Fred smacked his lips. 'Sure! Give me a call about it later, uh?'

'I'll do that,' promised George, and went about his business. He sold three policies insuring against damage caused by satellites, two endowments and one to an old man who was terrified of cremation. George was proud of the last because the company had their own burial ground and, as far as they were concerned, the premiums were sheer profit. When he arrived back home he was pleasantly tired after a profitable day.

Martha started in on him as soon as he had eaten.

'They have everything delivered,' she said. 'I managed to catch the delivery wagon and the man told me that they order everything by mail.'

'Mail?' George looked blank. 'Why don't they use the phone?'

'I don't know,' she said grimly. 'The man said that everyone at the store talks about it. They are the only mail-order customers they have in town.' She nodded as though her worst suspicions had been confirmed. 'I found out their name too. Randall. It isn't in the phone book.'

'It could be a private listing,' said George, but the way he said it left no doubt that he didn't think it possible. A private listing yes, but who would bother to write a letter when they could just use the phone? He told Martha what he had learned from the estate agent.

'I don't like it,' she said when he had

finished. 'It isn't natural.'

'They're old,' he defended. 'Old people aren't as spry as younger ones. Maybe that's why they haven't got a car or a television set.' He didn't argue about the television set. If Martha had said they didn't have one then that was that. Aerial or no aerial she would have been able to recognise one by smell alone. Martha, to put it politely, was sharp.

'Fiddlesticks! My folks are old but they have all those things. Lots of people are but they have cars and use phones. If you ask me it isn't natural the way they're going on.'

He hadn't asked her but it made no difference. George knew that he would be plagued by the next door neighbours until Martha's curiosity was assuaged to the full, and, despite his initial reluctance, he found himself becoming intrigued.

Maple Avenue was a perfect representation of its type. A row of houses filled with people of much the same income-bracket and all adhering firmly to a recognised pattern of living. The Randalls had broken that pattern and so, merely because of that, they stuck out like a sore thumb.

The more George thought about it the more his imagination began to work. A firm follower of the television soap operas, a hungry seeker after vicarious thrills via the popular press, he, like all his class and most of his race, suffered from frustration and utter boredom. The Randalls, harmless as they must obviously be, yet presented a safe, snug little problem in detection. Who were they? What were they? Why didn't they use the benefits of modern civilisation?

George determined to find out.

* * *

Martha's sister had married a banker and so it was inevitable that the sole child of their marriage, a son, should work in a bank. That it happened to be the Union Bank was, George thought, a deserved coincidence. He invited the young man to lunch and, over a meal began to delicately pump for information.

'It's a matter of business, John,' he

explained. 'I'm figuring on selling the Randalls a big policy and, naturally, I'd like a hint of their financial background.' He paused, waiting for John to first nibble, then swallow the bait.

'Well . . . ' John seemed reluctant to betray the confidence of his clients. George was quick to sense it and even quicker to apply just the right amount of pressure.

'It's not as if I were a stranger, John,' he beamed. 'I could find out myself, of course, but I thought that you could save me a little time.' He managed to give the appearance of hurt dignity. 'After all, it's not as though my business wasn't respectable.'

John nodded. Selling, no matter what product, was classed a little higher than banking and just under the medical services for the simple reason that the average salesman earned more than the average bank clerk and slightly less than the average doctor. That, to any right-minded man, made George's request both reasonable and right.

'They've got triple-A Dunn and Bradstreet rating,' John said, and having said so much, proceeded to say more. 'We pay most of their bills by bankers order but sometimes they send for some cash.'

'Much cash?'

'No, not much, about what would be expected for small items and general expenses. Tips and so on.'

'So financially they are a good risk.' George nodded as though he had found out all he wanted to know. 'You must have handled their account for some time then?'

'No.' John hesitated. 'As a matter of fact we haven't. Their account was sent to us from head office.' He hesitated again. 'From their file it seems that every time they move their account is routed via head office to a local branch.'

'Reasonable.' George shrugged as if it were of no importance. 'How about income?'

'Paid into head office. I saw one of the cheques, it had got caught up in their file by mistake, it was from the Universal Drug Company and it was pretty big.'

'Shares perhaps?'

'No. More like a pension I would say. I've seen share-cheques before.' John stared at his uncle. 'You understand that all this is confidential?'

'Naturally.' George hesitated before asking the final question. 'Do they move often?'

'The Randalls?' John shrugged. 'Hard to tell but I'd say yes. We haven't got the complete file, remember, only what head office chooses to send us.' He looked at his watch. 'If there's anything else . . . ?'

There wasn't and George said so. He lingered over his coffee after John had gone and, because he had time to spare, made one more call.

* * *

He was plausible, smooth, very eager to help and utterly baffled when the man at the electricity offices regretfully informed him that Mr. Randall did not and had not ever owed them money.

'But that's unbelievable!' George was more than startled, he was shocked. For a family in this day and age not to use electricity was as incredible as an eighteenth century gentleman who never spent money on candles. When he came to think about it the man obviously thought so too.

'Maybe they have their own generator?' he suggested. 'Are you certain that Mr. Randall asked you to pay his bill?'

'He certainly asked me to pay a bill for him,' said George. He grinned. 'Still, if they don't use your current it can't be for that, can it?'

Outside the offices he paused to stare into the display window. It was filled with the essentials of modern living. Irons, washing machines, refrigerators, ovens, fans, heaters, bulb-lights and strip-lights, door chimes, blankets, radios, recorders, television sets, videophones, all and every one operated by electricity. To live without all or most of them was unthinkable.

And yet the Randalls used no commercial electricity.

George decided to go and see them.

* * *

There was no bell. Or rather there was a push-button but it didn't seem to be working. He waited for a while then, as nothing happened, rapped on the door with his bare knuckles. The impact bruised his tender skin and he was sucking his fingers when the door opened and a woman stared at him.

She was normal. She was dressed in a shapeless garment of rusty black and her face had a peculiar lost expression but she was human. George took his hand from his mouth, smiled, and went into his prepared routine.

Because he was a salesman and because he was good at his job he was inside the house with the door closed behind him before the woman had a chance to protest at the intrusion. Then, just as he suspected she would, she went to find her husband.

Alone, George took a quick look at the lounge.

It looked like a museum.

The furniture had gone with the house, obviously, but the furnishings hadn't. The curtains were of heavy brocade, embroidered and tasseled and looped back with plaited ropes. The chairs had little lace mats resting on their backs and arms. A great brass bowl held some green-leafed plant and, beside it was a swollen thing with a glass chimney and a round glass shade. George was still trying to figure out just what it was for when the door opened and the Randalls, both of them, entered the room.

The man, in his own way, was a carbon copy of the woman. Both had the same lost expression. Both wore ludicrous clothing, that of the man even more noticeable than that of the woman with its narrow trousers, the narrow lapelled coat, the collared shirt and thin tie. Both seemed almost as if they were terrified of their visitor. George tried to put them at their ease.

'Mr. Randall?' He beamed and held out his hand. 'I'm representing the Acme Insurance Company and I think that I have something here which will interest you.' He had no real hope of selling any insurance but the excuse had served to get him into the house. Mr. Randall cleared his throat with a dry, rasping sound, and looked at his wife.

'Insurance?'

'Yes. You know what that is, don't you?'

'Of course.' Randall gestured to a. chair and turned to his wife. 'A glass of wine, dear?' He smiled as she left the room. 'I'm afraid that you're wasting your time Mr.?'

'Prentice. George Prentice. Call me George.'

'Very well, then. George. As I said I'm afraid that you're wasting your time. We have no real need for insurance at all.'

'Nonsense!' George was really hurt. 'Everyone needs insurance. To be frank, Mr. Randall, a man is a fool if he doesn't buy all the coverage he can afford. What if you should die?'

'Die?' Randall frowned as if the word should mean something but he had forgotten just what. His face brightened. 'Oh, that! We don't have to worry about that, either of us.' He looked oddly at George. 'Pardon me, Mr. Prentice, but is there a carnival in town?'

'George,' corrected George absently. 'Carnival? No, why do you ask?'

'Well, your clothes.' Randall seemed a

little embarrassed. 'You must admit that they are rather unusual. I wondered . . . '

George wasn't shocked but he was hurt a little. Personally he considered his lemon blouse and green slacks with the maroon sash and matching sandals as rather conservative. Not a bit like the polka dot styles the younger set were wearing or the striped patterns favoured by the manual workers. If anyone in town was oddly dressed it was the Randalls. He was about to say so when Mrs. Randall returned with the wine.

It was good wine. It had a rich, fruity body to it and was surprisingly potent. Sipping it, George wondered why the wine he bought from the store never tasted anywhere near as good. He asked Randall what it was.

'Elderberry,' said the man. 'Mary made a batch last year, she's good at that sort of thing.' He held up his glass and looked at the dark red fluid. 'I must say it's some of the best she's ever made.'

'It's wonderful!' George held out his glass for more. 'Now, Mr. Randall, about this insurance of yours. You say that you are already insured against death?'

'Yes.' He glanced at the woman. 'I don't think that either of us need worry about that.'

'Good coverage.' George nodded. The wine had gone to his head a little but, even so, he remembered who he was and why he had come. He saw no reason to waste an opportunity. 'I'd like to have a look at those policies of yours, Mr. Randall. I might be able to suggest something to your advantage. Quite often I've been able to convert an old policy into a new one with great advantage to the policyholder. Do you have them at hand?'

'Policies?' Randall blinked and again smiled in his secret way. 'I believe so. Mary, dear, could you get them for Mr. Prentice.' He smiled at George as she scuttled from the room. 'I doubt if you'll find anything of the slightest interest in them. Personally I doubt if we'll ever gain anything from them.'

'You can never tell,' said George sententiously. 'Anything can happen and it usually does when least expected. Take a claim I had to settle last week. Debris from a satellite smashed the roof of a house. A billion to one chance, you say, but it happened. Fortunately my client was insured and so suffered no loss.' He stretched out his hand as the woman entered the room. 'These the policies? Thank you.'

He took them and leaned back in his chair as he studied them. They were old, the paper yellow and brittle with age. Gently he unfolded them, marvelling at the thick, black-letter type and the generally poor layout of the text. He jotted down the name of the company and the numbers of the policies in his memo-book, and then idly scanned them for relevant information.

He boggled at what he read!

The policies were both the same. They were of a single-premium type with a ridiculously low payout value. From what he gathered they had been given away on receipt of the premium and the signed promise to subscribe for the following ten years to a particular newspaper. There were blanks, now filled in, for the name and age of the beneficiary and the date of the policy was in more of the ridiculous black-letter type.

Carefully he folded them and handed them back. He finished his wine and promised to look into the matter for them. Randall demurred but George waved aside his objections.

'No trouble, no trouble at all. I only live next door so I can pop in at any time.' He pretended to think about it. 'Look, I'll check up and drop in tomorrow evening. We can talk about it then.'

He smiled and nodded and walked out of the house. He was still affected a little by the wine and it wasn't until he was almost home that it struck him. He halted, one hand half-outstretched to the lock-plate, and stared at the silent house he had just left.

The date on the policies had been 1887. The age of Randall had been 45 and that of his wife five years less. If what he had read had been the truth that made the both of them about a hundred and seventy years old!

He didn't talk much to Martha that

evening but, by next morning, George had convinced himself that he had made a mistake. He blamed the wine, that and the unusual furnishings of the lounge and the odd clothing of the Randalls. Anyone could have noticed a wrong date or age and, the more he thought about it, the more convinced he became that he had misread the policies.

Down at the office he made the routine check and received his second shock.

'These policies went out with the Ark,' said Edwards, the check-file clerk. He stared at the memo George had passed to him. 'Where did you dig them up, in a junk shop?'

'No, why?'

'Because they aren't worth the paper they're printed on. It was a newspaper stunt, one of several they tried to boost circulation, and I believe they actually paid out a few of them. They had their own cover, of course, but the policies lapsed when the newspaper went out of circulation.' He handed back the memo. 'Someone's trying to play you for a sucker,' he grinned. 'Hope they didn't take up too much of your time.'

'Not too much,' said George. He was bitter both at himself and at the Randalls. Obviously they had passed him a couple of heirlooms, probably taken out by Randall's parents, and the more he thought about it the more upset he became. The joke was in the worst of taste because it had both wasted his time and, more important, made him look foolish before the check-file clerk.

He determined to see the Randalls and complain.

Pressure of work kept him until dusk and it was almost dark before he was able to knock on the door of his neighbour's house again. As before the woman opened it and, as she did so, a flood of soft yellow light streamed out from over her shoulder.

'Good evening, Mrs. Randall,' said George heartily. 'Sorry I'm late but I had a little trouble checking your policies.'

She stared at him without the slightest trace of recognition.

'You remember me,' he urged. 'I called to see you yesterday. I'm your neighbour.'

'Are you?' She still didn't seem to recognise him but, with true feminine helplessness, allowed him to enter the house while she fetched her husband.

The lounge looked just the same but this time George found out what the glass-chimnied thing was for. It was a lamp, the source of the soft yellow light, and his nose wrinkled to the rank smell of burning oil.

Randall didn't know him either.

He stood by his wife, their hands defensively clasped together, and stared at George as if he were a lunatic or a criminal.

'Look,' said George slowly. 'I called on you yesterday. I live next door. You showed me some insurance policies. Now do you remember?'

'I've never seen you before in my life,' said Randall stiffly. He seemed nervous. George sighed and tried again.

'I sat in that chair and we talked for quite a while. Why, you even gave me some of your wine, elderberry, you said it was.' He stared at their blank expressions. 'Damn it all! I was here, I tell you!'

'I don't know who you are,' said Randall, 'or why you are dressed like that, but you have never been inside this house before. I have never offered you wine nor spoken with you. I suggest you leave now before I am forced to send for the police.'

'Why send for them,' said George sarcastically. 'Why not phone?'

'Phone?' Randall glanced at his wife. 'Do you know what he is talking about, dear?'

'Forget it,' said George disgustedly. 'You don't know what a phone is, you don't use electricity, you wear clothes straight from a museum.' He slapped his pocket and grinned. 'Well, I can prove you wrong in one thing. I have here the numbers of your policies. Now, I couldn't have got those without you showing them to me, could I?' He produced the memo and handed it to Randall. 'Will you check?'

He waited while the woman scuttled out of the room to fetch the papers and, when she returned, he waited as Randall checked his slip against the numbers.

'Well? Am I right?'

'They match,' admitted Randall. 'But that proves nothing.'

'It proves that I've seen the policies,' pointed out George. He took a deep breath. 'They are your policies, aren't they?'

'Yes.'

'I see.' The joke was wearing thin and George was losing his temper. 'Just when did you take them out?'

'About five years ago.' Randall moistened his lips with the tip of his tongue and George suddenly became aware that the couple were afraid of him. 'It seemed a good investment at the time but I don't think we'll need it now.'

'No? Why not?' They didn't answer and George didn't waste time. 'I don't know what your game is,' he said grimly, 'but it isn't funny. I'm a respectable businessman and entitled to common courtesy. If you took out those policies five years ago that would make your age about fifty. Right?'

'Yes.'

'And it would make the date . . . 1892. Right?'

'Of course.' Randall looked at him as though George were something from an asylum. 'What date did you think it was?'

And that was that.

⋆ ⋆ ⋆

He had argued, of course, but it had been a waste of time. Randall had insisted that they had never before met. He had insisted that the date was 1892. George was used to stubbornness, he had met and overcome men who emulated mules in that respect, but he had finally had to admit defeat. Because Randall had been telling the truth as he knew it and, the more George though about it, the more fantastically logical it became.

Quite literally the Randalls were living in a mental world of the remote past.

The intriguing part was why?

George began to do some investigating.

It wasn't too hard and yet, at the same time, it wasn't too easy. For anyone else it would have been impossible but the web of the intermeshed insurance companies had spread to cover every man, woman and child in the Western Hemisphere. George had access to the blacklists, the accident prones, the group analyses and the statistical extrapolations of every age group and income-bracket there was.

And he had the starting point of the original policies.

Sam and Mary Randall had lived and worked in a small town during the years of 1875 to 1892. They had worked for a chemical firm, which later had expanded into the Universal Drug Company. They had later moved to another small town towards the west coast.

A fire insurance policy had been taken out by their late firm to cover their new home.

They had lived there ten years and then moved again.

Another policy had then been taken out for the same reason and by the same firm.

And so it went on.

It took a long time and George kept the check-file clerks in a state of wonderment as to his sanity, but the investigation paid off. The Randalls, like it or not, were around a hundred and seventy years old and were the same people who had taken out the original life insurance. And that, incidentally, was the only life insurance they had ever taken out.

George wasn't dumb and he had a good imagination. He was in a business that dealt with probability and statistical analysis and was as able to extrapolate as well as the next man. So the logical assumption of what he had learned didn't upset him in the least.

Immortality.

Or, if not exactly that, then something very much like it. He had seen the Randalls and, though they looked old, yet they only looked as old as they had been, not as old as they should be. People had aged more back in the nineteenth century. Since then modern medicine and hygiene had lifted the life expectancy to almost double what it had been a hundred and seventy years ago. They merely looked as old as people of their age did when they had taken or done whatever it was that had kept them alive when they should have been dead. The extra years hadn't aged them at all.

Would a thousand?
Would ten thousand?
Would a million?

George was still thinking about it when his door opened and a man walked into his office. He entered unannounced which was bad, and he walked with an innate assurance which was worse. George could recognise authority when he saw it and he knew that he was looking at it now. The man wasted no time.

'You are George Prentice and you live next door to the Randalls on Maple Avenue. You have been making some investigations as to your neighbours. Why?'

'Who are you?'

'Does that matter?' The man smiled with a hint of iron beneath the velvet. 'If I tell you that I'm connected with the Universal Drug Company, will that help you? If I also tell you that I'm in the position of being your boss, will that help you more?' He leaned forward across the desk. 'Please understand me, Mr. Prentice. I wish you no harm. I cannot force you to answer my questions but, if by so doing, you find yourself out of employment, blame yourself, not me. Well?'

George told him.

Strangely enough the man wasn't surprised. He listened and, when George had finished, he nodded as if admiring a neat piece of deduction.

'You are right. The Randalls are potentially immortal. Naturally you are thinking of acquiring the same immortality for yourself. If you are, then please believe me when I tell you to dismiss the thought completely from your head.'

'Why should I?' George hadn't really thought it out as far as that but, when he heard the other make the suggestion, he realised what he had discovered.

'You have seen the Randalls,' reminded the man. 'Hasn't anything struck you as strange about the way they live?'

'Of course. It was that strangeness which first made me suspicious.'

'Exactly. Would you care to live in the same way?' He continued before George had a chance to answer. 'You see, the type of immortality which they have was discovered quite by accident. The . . . serum, was perfected late in the nineteenth century and the Randalls acted as guinea pigs. I won't go into details but if I tell you that the serum, though it isn't a serum, has the power of restoring the body cells to the status quo after a period of twenty-four hours, you may know what I mean. All the cells, Mr. Prentice. In effect the process of aging and degeneration of the entire body is wiped out during each day.'

He paused. 'Memory, Mr. Prentice, comes beneath the heading of cellular damage.'

* * *

It was, when you came to think about it, obviously simple and perfectly logical. Each day the Randalls aged a little and, each night, that age was wiped out by the serum. The trouble was that their memories of that day were also wiped out. Memory is cellular damage. That damage was erased. With the erasure went the memories of the previous day.

'Yes,' said the man gently. 'It's rather horrible to contemplate, isn't it? The serum itself was one of those discoveries made in the search for something quite different. We were after a cancer cure at the time, I believe, at least the founders of the firm were, and no one was more surprised than they to see what had happened. The Randalls remained static. They could not remember anything after about a week past the injection. It took that long for the serum to take hold. In effect they are frozen in time and each new day brings bewildering terrors. How would you feel if, each day, strangely dressed men spoke to you of things you knew nothing about? Wouldn't you tend to remain isolated? Wouldn't you be afraid and upset all the time?'

George nodded. His imagination was working and he could see all the flaws and snags. What was the good of living forever if, in effect, all you did was to relive one day after the other?

'We look after them, naturally,' said the man. 'They are pensioners of the firm and, though we can never undo the harm we have caused them, yet we try to make things easier for them. One day, perhaps, we'll find the antidote and give them the natural ending they should have had years ago.' He rose and smiled down at George.

'I'm sure that you'll respect my confidence. After all, who would believe you if you told them?' He smiled again and then as abruptly as he had arrived, he left.

George sat and did some heavy thinking.

Immortality was out, he didn't want it at that price, but wasn't there something else? He smiled. There was. With the memory setup they had it would be the simplest thing in the world to sell them fresh insurance each day. Simple because they would forget that they had ever bought a policy from him before. And, with his business skill and knowledge of their ways, he would be able to talk them into everything from endowment to earthquake, drain-damage to deterioration. He wouldn't live forever, but he would be rich!

But he wasn't.

By the time he managed to call, the Randalls had moved and he never did find out where they went.

3

Sleeve of Care

The woman was small, faintly ridiculous in her odd assortment of dress and accessories. Mousy hair straggled from beneath a hat which had been new the last fashion but one. A shapeless coat was belted around a shapeless figure and thick stockings tried their best with hopeless legs. She stared at a thick, old-fashioned wedding ring and twisted it with nervous fingers.

'I want to find my husband,' she said. 'I want you to find him.'

Sam Henricks sighed. There was no money here, no excitement, not even the possibility of a satisfied client recommending him to others. A waste of time.

'Have you tried the police?' he said, and managed to keep the impatience from his voice. He smiled. 'Private investigators cost money; the police will work for free.'

The woman did not smile. 'I have money,' she said. 'A little. I want you to find my husband.'

'I see.' Sam pulled a scratch pad towards him and toyed with a pencil. He waited while the woman rummaged in her purse and produced a thin billfold. She opened it and took out a thin sheaf of bills. Sam could almost smell the odour of camphor as she waved them before him.

'I haven't much,' she said uncertainly. 'I'm not rich . . . but it's all I have.'

Sam counted the bills with an experienced eye, mentally shrugging as he assessed the amount. The woman was a fool. She had probably scraped the bottom of her financial barrel to pay for something that the police, the Salvation Army, the Church, would have done for nothing. For a moment he was tempted to refuse to handle the case, then remembered his rent, his bills, and the state of his bank account. He shrugged again, physically this time, and reached out for the money.

'I think it will do. Now, if you will let me have some details, please.' He poised the pencil. 'Name?'

'Jud Everet Johnson.' Like her clothes, her voice was colourless, whispering from between bloodless lips, giving him the information that made a man.

Fifty-six years of age. Five feet nine inches tall. Ten stone five pounds in weight. Wears thick, horn-rimmed spectacles. Stoop shouldered. Gray hair, thin on top and cropped back and sides. Never wore a hat. Dressed in blue serge, rather worn and a little shiny. Black shoes, blue shirt, red and blue tie. Cheap metal wristwatch. No rings. Worked as a clerk and had been with the same firm twenty years. No children. No hobbies. Nothing.

Sam jotted down the framework, stared at the thin lined face on a photograph the woman gave him, and tried to clothe the naked bones with warm, breathing flesh.

'No hobbies?' He stared at the woman. 'Do you mean that literally?'

He read the classics, the cheap layman's translations. He played cards sometimes, whist, rummy, a little cribbage. He had once kept goldfish and used to own a motor cycle. No hobbies.

'Friends?'

None that she didn't know about. A few people from the office, a couple of neighbours, a few men and women acquaintances at the whist drive. No friends.

'Women friends?'

Impossible!

'Money?'

None. A joint savings account with her as the financial manager doling out a strict budget for newspapers, cigarettes, lunches and fares. No money.

And yet the man had disappeared.

Sam thinned his lips as he stared down at his notes. An ageing, apparently normal man. One of millions. Colourless, insignificant, in fair health and mental stability, had left for work as he had done a thousand times before. Had walked from his neat, mortgaged, semi-detached house in a respectable suburb — and vanished.

And his wife wanted him back.

He stared at her, lounging back in his chair and studying her with impersonal eyes. Young once, obviously. Attractive once, perhaps. No children. No personality. A woman for whom a man had turned himself into a workhorse. Going to work, coming home, going to work, coming home, forcing himself into a mould, a rigid routine, a complete negation of all he had ever wanted or hoped to be. For how long?

'We've been married for thirty years,' she said with quiet pride. 'Jud was a little wild when I first met him, but he settled down well and turned out to be a good husband.' She dabbed at her washed-out eyes. 'I can't understand what could have happened to him.'

'Perhaps . . . ' Sam hesitated, knowing how ridiculous the question would seem to her. 'Perhaps your husband wanted to disappear? I . . . '

'Nonsense!' Anger glowed for a moment in her faded eyes. 'We were happy, with a nice home and a steady job. Why should he want to run away and leave it all behind?'

A hundred reasons, Sam thought

grimly. A younger woman, perhaps, or one not so eager to obey the conventions. Vibrant flesh and a transitory youth again, instead of the cold, regulated dispensation of frigid favours. Perhaps a glimpse of what he had become and a recoiling from it. Perhaps anything.

'I'll contact you when I have investigated,' he said formally. 'I have all the details, I think. Your address, the address of your husband's place of business. Savings account, friends, background, personal history.' He rose and held out his hand. 'Don't worry, madam. I'll find him.'

She smiled at that, a twisting of her lips and a gleam of something, not humour, in her eyes. Primly, she gathered up her handbag, adjusted her coat, nodded, and left the office.

Sam wished that he could get the taste of her from his mouth.

* * *

It was routine, of course; it always was. First to the missing persons bureau, where he did for money what she could have done free — and found that she had already done it. To a big, tired, cynical sergeant with numerous files and a wide-flung web of contacts. A man who had spent most of his life looking for an answer — and still not finding it.

'Jud Everet Johnson?' The sergeant nodded as he riffled through the pages of his ledger. 'I remember, now. A missing husband case.' He squinted down at his book. 'Gone ten days now.' He stared at Sam. 'What's your interest?'

'I've been asked to find him.'

'So you think you can succeed where we failed?'

'No.' Sam found cigarettes and passed one to the big man. Blue smoke rose between them like incense to the Gods of routine and the inexplicable. He smiled. 'You know how it is. The woman is impatient, can't even begin to guess why it happened to her. Wants her husband back again so she can restore her nice, quiet, orderly world to untarnished respectability. You know how it is.'

'I know.' The sergeant dragged at his cigarette.

'You find anything?'

'Plenty.' The sergeant reached towards a file. 'He isn't dead, or if he is we haven't found him. He isn't a hospital case, either physical or mental, and he wasn't in an accident. He hasn't been arrested and he isn't wanted for any crime.' The big man shrugged. 'There isn't any law which says that a man must live with his wife. That comes after she gets a court order for maintenance and he refuses to pay — and he can always get out by paying.'

'What with?' Sam flicked ash from his cigarette. 'Did he have private money? A secret woman who might be keeping him?'

'Not that we know.'

'So he just vanished without any obvious reason?'

'That's about it.' The sergeant sighed as he replaced the file. 'It happens all the time. We'll find him.'

'Are you sure about that?'

'The percentages are sure. More than a thousand people disappear every week. They just vanish — or try to. Most of them we trace pretty soon. Some are suffering from amnesia, others are running from their responsibilities, most just can't take it. Something snaps and off they go.' He shrugged. 'A few take the trouble to plan their disappearance; we know what's happened to them, even though we don't know where they are.'

'But this case wasn't like that,' protested Sam. 'Jud didn't sneak out a few clothes, hide a little money, have friends his wife didn't know about.' He remembered the woman and shuddered. 'I'll bet he couldn't cross the road without her knowing when and why. They weren't a couple, they were one unit, and she was the boss.'

'All the more reason for his going.'

'Perhaps, and yet a man like that wouldn't know the first thing about it. He'd try to be clever, and give himself away. No, if you ask me, this is another one of those mysteries. You know what I mean?'

'Who better?' The sergeant stared at his ranked files. 'We find most of them. Sometimes it takes years, but we find them. Some we never find. Some just

— vanish. No reason. Nothing. They just disappear.'

'Like the man who walked around the horses?' Sam nodded. 'I'll keep in touch,' he promised. 'No objections?'

'Why should there be?' The sergeant shrugged. 'You've got to eat.' He didn't ask why, but his expression did, the inevitable contempt of the professional for the amateur, the skilled man for the bungler. Sam didn't let it annoy him.

Tramping then. Walking from door to door, from office to office, asking, questioning, smiling and polite. Clothing a skeleton with flesh, filling in the gaps, searching for the one thing that could have made a humdrum clod kick over the traces and cut free from the habit pattern of thirty years.

A café, a waitress who remembered, and a fact.

'Mr. Johnson?' She frowned at the photograph. 'Yes, I remember him. A quiet man, never tipped, but always patient. Favourite food? Well, he nearly always had cheese on toast or spaghetti. Newspaper? *The Tribune* I think and two cups of coffee, one with and one after his meal.'

Fact: Liked cheese and spaghetti. Two cups of coffee and read *The Tribune*.

The office with furtive-eyed men and simpering girls. A man who remembered, another fact.

'Jud? Hell, yes, I know him. Quiet type. Never one for a drink. Used to have a sly bet sometimes. I used to put it on for him. Win? Sometimes, but not often, just about enough to stay even. Women? Not that I know of. Conversation? Nothing special. Home and garden, wife and work. A dull type. No guts.'

Fact: Gambled a little, cautious, timid, conventional.

From the office to the library, where a mannish woman stared at the photograph, flipped a stack of cards, and frowned at the list of book borrowings.

'Pretty much of a pattern. You can tell a lot from what a man reads, you know. Moore and Plato, Homer and Wells, Sabatini and Clarke. Kinsey? Certainly not! Mr. Johnson wasn't that kind of a man.'

Fact: Intelligent — at least in his public literature. His private?

The postman shook his head.

'Few letters. Nothing in plain seal. No magazines, parcels or foreign mailings. Photographs? Not that I know of.'

Fact: Little outside contact.

And so on. Talks with curious neighbours who licked mental lips as they scented scandal. Talks with the local doctor, the police, the man who sold newspapers and the one who sold cigarettes. Talks with the people who served behind counters, kept bar, punched tickets. A row of faces, each with masked eyes and guarded tongue. Dozens of them.

And at the end?

Nothing.

* * *

Sam grunted as he unlocked the door of the small house he had so far managed to keep from the jaws of his creditors.

Tiredly, he eased himself inside and sighed with relief as he slipped the shoes from his aching feet. Madge called to him from the kitchen where she hummed as she worked with iron and heaps of freshly laundered clothing.

'Sam?'

'Yes, dear?'

'Hungry?'

'No. I ate out.' He relaxed against the worn upholstery. 'Where's Tony?'

'Playing in the garden.' Madge wiped her hands as she came into the living room. 'You're late today.'

'A case.' He didn't explain or tell her what; and she didn't ask.

'Coffee?'

'Please.' A mirror hung over the mantelpiece and he stared at his own reflection as he sipped the coffee, grateful for its warm sweetness. Grimly he stared back at himself, a brown-haired, brown-eyed man, no longer young, and yet not old. Lines of worry searing once smooth cheeks, more lines creasing his forehead, the corners of his eyes, accentuating the bitterness of his mouth.

A tired face. A disillusioned face. The face of a man who had seen too much and done too little about it. An ordinary face. The face of a man about to vanish?

Sam sighed and set down his empty cup.

Tony came in then, vibrant and eager with the wonderful health of youth, his voice high and shrill with the tones of childhood.

'Dad!'

'Yes, son?'

'Freddie Blake's got two new fish, and can I have some more, tomorrow, please?'

'More fish?' Sam forced himself to be patient. 'You can only put so many in the tank, you know. If you overcrowd them they'll die.'

'Gosh, Dad.' Tony ran over to the small aquarium, bright with its lights and tropical fish, standing in the corner of the room. He stared at it, his brown eyes following the languid, lazy motions of the angels and mollies, the swordtails and zebras, the slow and stately snails and the wriggling tuberfix worms. 'Dad!'

'Yes, son?'

'Something's wrong, Dad. Look!'

Reluctantly, Sam heaved himself upright from the chair and joined his son. Together, they stared at the miniature, aqueous world behind the glass. 'What is it, Tony?'

'That fish, dad. See?' A little finger touched the glass. 'It's not moving.'

'Perhaps it's just resting?'

'It was like it this morning, and, it doesn't seem to have moved all day.' Tony stared worriedly at his father. 'Is it dead?'

'I don't think so.' Sam lifted the lid of the aquarium and picking up a slender planting stick from a shelf, prodded gently at the fish. Startled, it moved with a flurry of fins, its mouth opening and closing as if scolding them for disturbing its rest, then settled down to the gravel bottom.

'It still isn't moving, Dad, not like the others. Could it be ill?'

'We'll see tomorrow, Tony.'

'But suppose it's ill, Dad?'

'Then we'll have to take it out of the tank.'

'Suppose it died?'

'We'll have to take it out before it affects the other fish.'

'Shouldn't we take it out now, Dad? Suppose it died in the night.'

'We'll leave it for tonight. If it isn't moving as it should in the morning we'll take it out then.' Sam smiled down at his son. 'We don't want it hurting the others, do we?'

'No, Dad.' Tony turned and immediately forgot the problem of the sluggish fish. 'Tell me a story.'

'Not tonight, son.' Sam tried not to feel guilt at his refusal, and Madge, sensing his weariness, moved purposefully towards their son.

'Daddy's tired tonight, Tony. Some other time.'

'Gosh, mum!'

'Now, now, Tony! And just look at that time! Bed now.'

'Must I?'

'Yes. It's late and you'll be too tired for school tomorrow. Hurry now.'

'All right, then.'

Silence and the bumping of a small body as it ran upstairs and donned pyjamas. Then a shining little face and a mop of tousled hair, a small body vibrant with life and freedom from care. Lips raised for a goodnight kiss.

' . . . 'night, Dad.'

'Goodnight, son. Sleep well.'

Sam sighed as he watched his wife escort their son from the room and upstairs to his bed. Soon the little mind would be at rest; the deep, peaceful, utterly absorbing sleep of healthy youth would enfold the boy and he would awake tomorrow full of adventure and bright illusion.

Sam almost envied his son.

Madge came down after a while and sat beside him, not speaking, not doing anything, but fill a gap with her body and presence. For a while they sat there, each busy with their own thoughts; then, rising, she made coffee and handed him a steaming cup.

'Hard day, Sam?'

'Routine.' He spooned sugar and sipped at the scalding brew. 'Missing husband case.'

'The usual?'

'Not this time.' He pulled a sour face. 'No secret vices, no hidden women friends, no sticky fingers. Just a man walking out into the great wide world and dodging out of sight. Completely. Just as if he'd dug a hole and pulled the edges in after him.' He shook his head: 'It's weird.'

'Perhaps he lost his memory?' Madge leaned across and took his empty cup. 'An accident, amnesia, anything? You'll find him.'

'Perhaps.'

'Yes you will. You're a good detective.'

'Am I?' he shrugged. 'I can shadow a cheating wife or playboy husband, and I'm good at taking photographs through bedroom windows. I can even check a set of books and put a finger on the office boy who's been helping himself to the stamp money. Sometimes I'm lucky and can even find a man who doesn't really give a damn whether he's found or not. But this case has me beat.'

'Why, Sam?'

'It doesn't make sense, that's why.' Irritably, he lit a cigarette, dragging deep at the smoke and letting it plume in twin streams through his nostrils. 'Look at it. A man vanishes. Just like that. Just leaves home for work and never gets there. Why? Damn it, why?'

'There must be some reason.'

'Is there?' Sam scowled at the smouldering tip of his cigarette. 'I wish I knew what it was then. I've checked with the police and they know nothing of him. That rules out accident, amnesia, mental breakdown and fear of discovery for embezzlement. For thirty years Jud Johnson has lived like a machine, and up to ten days ago there was no reason to suspect that he wouldn't end his life the same way.' The end of his cigarette sent sparks showering from the edge of the fireplace as he flipped it towards the cold grate.

'I've checked every lead I can think of. I've fitted in the gaps and built up what the man was like — and still it doesn't make sense.'

'You're trying too hard,' said Madge quietly. 'How can you hope to know him after a day?'

'I know my trade, Madge.' Sam fumbled for a fresh cigarette, knowing that he was smoking too much and feeling too tired to worry about it. 'Give me a swindler or a man with secrets, and I can spot them and track them down. There's a pattern, a sort of cause-and-effect about it, but Jud doesn't fit in at all.' He snapped his lighter, swore when it didn't work, and took the match Madge silently offered.

'A man who has been ground down by a possessive wife. A man who still can find it within himself to dream. His reading proves that. Sheer escapism, the Utopias of Moore and Plato, the swash-buckling of Sabatini, the heroics of Homer, the future worlds of Wells and Clarke. He must have lived in a private hell, and yet probably thought that his life was normal and so didn't dream of doing anything about it. A man who took no chances, gambled because he thought it would make him popular at work, ate cheap food and read a conservative newspaper. A carbon copy of ten million others. The so-called backbone of respect-ability. The clods who make this world what it is, instead of what it could be. And then he vanishes — and no one knows why.'

'But surely you've just explained why,' Madge said. 'Ground down, dreaming, perhaps the books he read just showed him what he was missing and . . . ' She made a gesture with her hands. 'He just kept on walking.'

'Like Felix?' Sam shook his head. 'I traced him from his home to where he bought a paper. Then to where he collected his daily ration of cigarettes. Those people remembered him; he'd been dealing with them for years. The ticket collector couldn't remember whether or not Jud had passed him, and we know that he never reached his office.'

'So he decided not to go to work after he'd bought his paper.' Madge shrugged., 'He'll turn up again. Men like that always do.'

'No,' said Sam slowly. 'I don't think that he will turn up. I don't think anyone will ever see Mr. Jud Johnson again.' He stared at his wife.

'There's something fishy about missing people,' he said. 'I don't mean those who just run out, or those who break down, or just have a gutful of routine and try to do something about it. Those people are explicable. We know what they do and why they do it. But there are others. Every week men and women disappear.

All over the world, in every civilized country, and some of those people are never found again.'

'You mean that they just vanish?' Madge frowned. 'But the police could find them . . . couldn't they?'

'No. The police can't find them. No one can find them.'

Sam spilled ash onto the carpet. 'It's one of those things. They just go. Poof! Like that. Without rhyme or reason. Hundreds of them every year.'

'But their papers, their employment cards?' Madge showed her bewilderment. 'They just can't *disappear*!'

'They do.'

'But why?'

'Why?' Sam shrugged. 'You're using the wrong word, honey. What's troubling me, is *how*?'

Silently he led the way up to bed.

* * *

The next morning he rose early, and before Tony could come down, had inspected the aquarium and decided to eliminate the sluggish fish. He did it with cold mercy, knowing that it would upset the boy to see it lying dead, and knowing, too, that it was more merciful to kill it than to leave it to suffer.

He was wiping his hands when Madge announced that breakfast was ready.

He ate quickly, his mind still tearing at the problem of the missing husband, and left the house before Tony had left for school. The day was bright, warm with summer and redolent with the scent of growing things. A good day.

The Salvation Army officer was kind, interested, but unable to tell him more than he knew. Sam leaned back in a chair as he gave the basic data.

'As far as I can gather, the missing man is fond of savouries, prefers coffee to tea, likes conservative things, whist, the classics and imaginative literature. The rest you, know.' He stared at the elderly man. 'How long?'

'Before we find him?' The officer shrugged. 'How can I tell? We may find him in one of our hostels; such things have often happened. Or he may come to us for guidance. In any case I shall notify our people, but frankly, I can offer little immediate hope. Sometimes it takes years to find a missing person.'

'And sometimes you never find them?'

'Yes.' The officer stared at Sam. 'Sometimes we never find them at all. No one ever finds them.' He rose. 'I shall send one of our people around to the wife. Poor soul, she will need all the comfort she can get in the bleak days to come. It is not easy to accept the loss of someone who has been the major part of your life.'

Sam nodded, a little surprised at the other's immediate thought of the wife, and felt a glow of shame as he remembered his own emotions when he had taken her money. He sighed, shaking hands as if the contact were something strange to him, and stepped from the cool office into the light of the bright sun.

He was finished.

He had done all he could, all he intended to do, and he had done nothing. The isolation of a few habit-patterns. The narrowing down of the moment and place at which the man had vanished. The elimination of any reasonable cause for the disappearance. Negative results. The knowing what Jud had *not* done, and now?

The great question of why and how. Particularly how.

How did a man vanish? Without money, clothes, friends. Without any of the things civilization regards as necessities. Vanishing as if he had stepped into a swamp, a quicksand, a hole. It is not easy for a man to vanish when a horde of clerks note his every move, his address, his employment. When the police watch every stranger and eyes stare, wedded to questioning brains. Who is he? Where does he come from? What does he do? No. It is not easy to step from life without leaving a trace.

And why?

Why leave everything gained from a lifetime of machinelike work? Sam stood on the street and breathed deeply at the warm air. What would make him leave his home and wife, his possessions and child? A great religious experience? A vision? A sudden desire to get away from it all? But he had a little money, some clothes, other things, and there was no hurry. He could always go. Tomorrow, the next day, the day after. There was no need for him just to vanish. Not yet.

He stepped from the kerb, his long legs thrusting at the concrete as he strode across the road, weaving expertly between traffic. One step, two; three . . .

And walked into darkness.

And walked into light again.

And stopped.

* * *

The street had vanished. The cars, the people, the drone of traffic, and the whisper of pedestrians. All gone. Instead . . .

A smooth floor. A tremendous sheet of blinding light facing him, soaring up from the floor to a fantastic height, brilliant with a cold, blue-white glow. Behind him another wall, tremendous like the first, smaller ones at each side, and above.

He looked up, then down, blinking as

his eyes flashed to the retinal after-image of glowing suns and glaring light. Almost he felt his skin prickle to that fierce glow, and as he moved in semi-blindness, his foot struck something on the floor and he stumbled, falling heavily to his knees.

A black man snarled at him. He had red-rimmed eyes and features haggard with brute incomprehension. He was naked, streaked with filth, his skin puckered with fantastic scars, and he rested on a bed of his own making.

Sam gulped and moved away.

It began to register then, and within his skull he felt his mind begin to twist with screaming questions. He had been walking across a crowded street, one moment safe and among familiar things; the next . . . ?

Madness?

He knew that it wasn't that. Whatever had happened, he hadn't suddenly gone stark, staring insane. This floor wasn't the product of delirium. He could feel it hard beneath his feet, and that man was real, and the walls, and the light. Wherever he was, he was really here, in the flesh, and if he was?

What had happened back on that crowded street?

A car could have hit him, thrown him down and cracked his skull so that things seemed not as they were. Tensely he examined his body, feeling his bones and muscles, then wearily dismissed the suggestion. He was healthy, in a strange place, and so sudden had been the transition that he felt no shock. Only a great wonder and a mounting sense of panic.

Where was he?

In a great room, that was obvious. A place of smooth, hard material, with one wall a glowing expanse of light, and the roof a searing brilliance. Grimly, Sam began to walk about the strange place, striding along the lighted wall, letting his fingers run over the smooth surface as he searched for a crack that would betray the presence of a door.

He didn't find a door, but he found something else.

People. Men and women, all sullen, all tired, all moving sluggishly over the smooth, once-clean floor. A pair of Chinese wandered past, their eyes glazed as if with opium. A swarthy pigmy chattered at him from where he sat on a heap of tubular, canelike reeds. Three sunken-eyed women staggered past as if drunk, reeling and swaying as they moved begrimed bodies over the floor. A bearded fakir whined at him and a brown islander with hair piled high on his scarred face strode past like a wooden statue.

And one white man.

He sat, head slumped on his chest, still dressed in shiny blue serge, his thin, grey hair rumpled and his eyes, as he stared at Sam, gleamed from behind the lenses of thick, horn-rimmed spectacles. He was about fifty-six, ten stone five, five feet nine, a clerk, married, very much so, a robot.

Mr. Jud Everet Johnson.

'Hello.' Sam sat down beside the elderly man. 'I've been looking for you.'

'Have you?' Jud spoke as if he had a mouthful of broken glass. He licked grey lips and dragged himself up from the reeds, which, like the pigmy, he sat on. 'Better get moving,' he said dully. 'Mustn't sit still too long.'

'Why not?' Sam paced beside the stumbling figure of the old man. 'What is this place?'

'Don't you know?'

'No. Do you?'

There was a dull fatigue in Jud's voice. A bleak indifference, a carelessness, a lack of curiosity. Staring at him, Sam felt a quick impatience and shook the thin shoulder beneath its covering of blue serge.

'What's the matter with you, man? Why did you run away from home? Where are we?'

'I don't know.'

'Listen,' said Sam tightly. 'You've been gone for ten days now. Have you been here all that time?'

'I don't know.' Jud licked his lips and staggered, his thin legs collapsing and his thin arms sprawling like the limbs of some crippled spider. Impatiently, Sam stooped over him, dragged him to his feet, sent his palm hard against the grey cheek.

'Answer me, damn you! Where are we?'

'I . . . '

A scream slashed through the thick air. A shriek as of a soul in eternal agony, a rending, heart-stopping sound, and the man Sam had seen first, bounded to his feet and ran, half-falling, down the room.

'What's the matter with him?' Sam glared at the scarred figure and shook the man at his side. 'Jud! What's all this about?'

'Tired,' croaked the thin man. 'Sleep. Mustn't stop. Keep moving.'

'Why?'

'Dangerous. Hurts. Vanish.'

He sagged again and Sam swore as he half-carried the thin figure towards a pile of reeds. Impatient or not, the thin man was in no condition to answer and Sam knew that if he wanted a quick answer, he would have to find it somewhere else. Leaving Jud on his heap of reeds, he made a quick examination of the great room.

Five hundred feet long by a hundred wide, and about the same high. All made of smooth, seamless material, hard and slick like glass. On the floor heaped masses of the strange reeds, thick, bamboo-like, spread in wild confusion. No doors. No water faucets. No sanitation — and fifteen people including himself.

Two blacks; two Chinese; four women, Mongolian and unattractive; one pygmy; one fakir; two Islanders; one Inuit; and the two white Caucasians. Fifteen people of varying race and colour, all but a couple of them moving slowly over the floor, all apparently drunk or doped, all staggering and looking in the last stages of exhaustion.

Sam stared at them, wondering why they were here, then stooped and picked up one of the reeds. The wall of the bamboo-like vegetation was thin and he tore off a piece, finding the interior filled with a pale red pulp. Cautiously, he tasted it, finding it tart and refreshing, with a combination taste of crushed pineapple and peach. The pulp seemed to quench his thirst and he stood, eating the pulp, frowning as he stared around.

Someone shrieked in agonized torment.

It was Jud, and Sam ran towards the staggering figure, steadying him as he was about to fall, and trying to force him to sit down. The elderly man resisted him with surprising strength, flailing his thin arms and lurching over the floor, his eyes closed and his mouth agape. Watching him, Sam knew what was wrong.

The man was tired. Dog tired. Almost asleep on his feet. Numbed and dull from sheer lack of sleep, and staring at the others he knew that the same thing affected them all. They were tired, that was all, nothing wrong that a good night's sleep couldn't cure. But if they were tired why didn't, they sleep? He was still thinking about it when the lights went out.

It was sudden, startling in its abruptness. One moment the wall and roof flared with too-bright brilliance, and the next the room was as dark as the inside of a sealed tomb. With the darkness came a peculiar sound, a sighing, the soft thud of bodies, a snore, and Sam knew that every person in the place but himself had immediately fallen asleep.

He couldn't sleep.

He wasn't tired, and his brain spun

with unanswered questions, and he sat in the darkness, staring into the darkness, feeling it all around him like soft black velvet, like a warm hand, silent, pressing, somehow ominous. And within him the panic began to mount with gibbering frenzy.

A sealed room. Men and women, all different, with strange food on the floor. A mysterious something that made them move so that they staggered from utter exhaustion. Darkness. Mystery. A man who had vanished and who was here. Himself, who had not vanished and who was here also.

Vanished!

Sam gulped as he stared into the darkness. Jud had disappeared — and now he was here. Could he have disappeared also?

'Madge!' he groaned. 'Tony!'

They would never understand. To them there was no reason in the entire world why he should walk out on them, and they were right. As right as Mrs. Johnson had been; as a thousand other men and women were, and yet mere rightness did not prevent mysterious disappearances. And yet they mourned those who had walked out on their business and who had never returned. Would never return. Could never return? He groaned in the darkness and one question of relative importance gave way to one of paramount importance.

Why was he here?

He was still thinking about it when the lights flashed on and a scattering of reeds fell with a soggy thud to the floor.

Immediately the people awoke and began to move. Some rested for a while, only to shriek with pain and fear, and stagger to their feet. Jud moaned, sat up, and Sam tore open one of the new-dropped reeds and thrust a mass of the red pulp against the thin man's lips.

'Wake up, Jud. Eat this — and talk.'

'Yes.' His sleep, short as it had been, had done the man good, and as he stared at Sam his eyes had lost most of their glaze. He swallowed and tried to smile.

'My name is . . . '

'I know your name,' Sam interrupted. 'I know all about you. Just answer my questions.'

'Yes?'

'Tell me. How did you get here?'

'I don't know.' Johnson frowned as he ate the red pulp. 'I'd just bought my paper, *The Tribune*, you know, and was crossing the street when, all of a sudden, I was in here.'

'I see. That was ten days ago then, maybe eleven now.' He looked at the man, remembering his choice of reading material, and fighting his own impatience to drag the information out of the elderly clerk. 'What do you know about this place?'

'Nothing.'

'What?'

'You asked me what I know,' reminded the other. 'I don't know anything.'

'But you've been here ten days. You must know.'

'I don't.' Johnson gestured around him. 'When I came here I thought something must be wrong, my head perhaps, overwork . . . ' He let his voice trail into silence and rose to his feet. 'We'd better move about.'

'Why?'

'If you don't keep moving you get — hurt. If you still don't move you — vanish.'

'Vanish?'

'Yes. There was a man here before you, a white man, a professor, I think. He was very tired and he wouldn't keep moving. He just vanished.' Johnson stared about him with heavy eyes. 'It's happened before, I think.'

'If you're tired why don't you sleep?'

'We can't. The other man told me that the only time you could sleep was when the lights went out.'

'And how often does that happen?'

'I don't know; it's only happened once since I've been here.'

Once in ten days! Sam swallowed as he began to grasp the picture. A sealed room with an assortment of races. Food falling from the roof. Lights that almost never went out. A strange force which made you move — or else. He grabbed at Johnson's shoulder.

'What is this? Where are we?'

'I don't know.'

'But you can guess, can't you? Damn

it, man. Tell me what you think.'

'I read a book once,' said Johnson slowly. 'A strange book. It was written by a man named Charles Fort.'

'I know who you mean,' snapped Sam. 'Well?'

'He had some interesting theories.' Johnson almost blushed. 'I don't say that I believe them for one moment, but they were interesting, very.'

'We are property.' Sam nodded. 'I've heard of the book. Well?'

'That was his theory. What you have just said. Fort reckoned that there might be other races watching us, perhaps even owning us. I've wondered . . . '

'Hogwash!' Sam said, and hoped that he was right. 'How would that explain this?' He gestured around the room. 'Are you trying to tell me that these mysterious 'other races' are scooping us up in the twinkling of an eye and are dumping us in this place like . . . like . . . ' He swallowed and sat down on a heap of reeds.

He knew what they were like.

He had known it all along, but perspective and an altered viewpoint had hidden what must be the truth. He stared at the others again. Black, white, yellow. Smooth and scarred, short-haired and long, big and small. A collection of divergent humanity.

A collection.

It would explain the room, the lights, the food. It would explain all the inexplicable disappearances, the senseless vanishings of staid and normal people, disappearing without trace, without rhyme or reason. It would explain too damn much.

He frowned, sitting on the heap of reeds, his mind busy with fantasy. A Mayfly was born, lived and died within a single day. To a Mayfly a day was a lifetime. To a Mayfly a man must seem to move awfully slowly. Other races, other time rates of metabolism. A day to them might be a long time, or a short time, depending on the viewpoint. A long time and men would appear to move slowly; a short time and men would seem to rush about with fantastic speed. Or perhaps the entire setup was different. A long day and a short night. A ten-day period of light and a one-day period of darkness.

Normal to them, but abnormal to men who needed to sleep a third of their time.

Sam felt sick.

He remembered his home and his boy and what they kept.

That fish looks ill, dad.

Were men 'fish'?

That one isn't moving, could it be ill?

A planting stick, a sudden flurry of motion, a soundless gasping of protest.

Better have that one out; it may spoil the rest.

A wriggling little body, wide eyes, a gaping mouth, a coldly merciful ending to what had appeared suffering. A taking from the tank, a vanishing? *Had that fish been tired or merely asleep?*

Pain slashed at him, a nerve-wrenching, mind-twisting stab of pure agony, and with his scream came a muscular reaction that sent him staggering across the floor. Sam gasped, noting that the pain vanished as soon as he moved, and grimly kept on moving as he wandered about the brightly lit room.

That brightly lit wall, a window through which alien eyes watched the antics of strange creatures with silent amusement? A worried youth wondering why his pets didn't move? A merciful being deciding that extended, and, therefore, abnormal motionlessness was a sign of sickness and death?

Sam didn't know.

He didn't want to think about it, but, as he moved slowly about the room, cursing himself for not sleeping when he'd had the chance, already feeling the strength-sapping fatigue which he knew waited for him, perhaps tomorrow, or the day after, or the day after that, he knew that he couldn't escape.

A collection.

In a tank.

With death waiting for any man or woman who didn't appear healthy.

How long could he manage to stay awake?

4

Little Girl Lost

They showed me the professor and then they told me what they wanted me to do. It wasn't a hard job, physically that is, but I could see that it would be more than wearing in other ways. I hesitated, they didn't seem to mind that, and then I took another look at the professor. That was easy because they had him hidden behind one-way glass.

He was dressing a little girl's hair. I could tell she was little and what he was doing by the way his hands hovered about three feet above the floor. He took his time about it, brushing, combing then weaving the hair into plaits. Two plaits tied with ribbon and he made hard work of the bows. When he had got them just right he kissed her on the forehead and tickled her under the arms, and then sent her out to play.

A nice, normal, everyday scene. The sort of thing every father does if he's lucky enough to have a little girl. The sort of thing every father has to do if he's unlucky enough to lose his wife. Nothing to it.

Only it was two in the morning in the centre of one of the most closely guarded places in the world. There was no brush, no comb, no ribbon.

And no little girl.

'It's his mind,' whispered the colonel. He didn't have to whisper, the professor couldn't have heard him had he shouted but he, like me, felt that he should lower his voice. 'To him she's still alive, his daughter I mean, and he can't accept the fact that she's dead.'

'When?'

'Six months ago. Hit and run driver, we never did find out who did it.'

'And the mother?'

'Died in childbirth.' The colonel stared through the one-way glass. Inside the soundproofed room the professor had sat down at the desk and was busy with pencil and paper. The colonel sighed and

I limped after him as he led the way back to his office.

Cottrell, the psychologist, was waiting for us and he passed cigarettes as we sat down.

'Well,' he said tightly, 'what's your reaction?'

'Do I have to have one?' I accepted a light from the colonel and blew smoke towards the desk light. 'I assume that you've a reason for keeping him where he is and I also assume that you've a reason for offering me a job.' I looked at the colonel. 'Incidentally, why me?'

'Security whitewashed you, the Air Force didn't want you, and you happen to resemble the professor when he was young.' Cottrell spoke before the colonel could answer. 'Also, the professor has a natural sympathy for the afflicted.'

I could have felt anger but I didn't. The accident that had blasted me out of the Air Force had also left me with a crippled leg and it isn't nice to remind a cripple of what he is. I guessed that Cottrell was sore at my getting the offer and said so. He shrugged.

‘Sorry, but that’s the answer. It’s important that the professor likes you. He doesn’t like me or any of us here. If you take the job you’ll have to be closer to him than his own skin and, above all, you mustn’t upset him in any way. It won’t be easy.’

‘I know that,’ I said. ‘But why? What’s the point?’

The colonel hesitated and I knew that I was treading on thin ice. Security ice, the sort which cracks if you so much as read the wrong newspaper. But the colonel was intelligent, he knew that no man can do a good job if he doesn’t know what he’s supposed to be doing. He took a chance.

‘The professor is important,’ he said slowly. ‘I can’t tell you how much or in just what way, but if I said that the future of this country depended on him I wouldn’t be exaggerating. He was working on . . . something . . . when his daughter was killed. It upset him. It almost ruined his mind so that, to us, he was useless. He only began to work again when he’d established his delusion.’ He looked at me through the smoke of his cigarette.

'He refuses to work here any longer. We can't make him. We can keep him here, yes, but only as an idiot. We don't want that. We want the genius of his mind and to get it we have to play things his way. We have to let him go so that he can work where he likes and when he likes, but we daren't let him go unprotected. So we want you to stay with him as a sort of friend and bodyguard. You keep him working, you pass on his findings and, above all, you keep him happy.' He sighed. 'I know that it seems crazy, but if you know a different answer I'd be glad to hear it.'

'I see.' My estimation of the professor had risen. 'Does he give any reason for wanting to leave here?'

'Yes.' Cottrell sounded bitter. 'He says that it's no place to bring up a young girl.' His laugh was more of a snort than anything else. 'He's perfectly right, of course, and, as we've got to humour his delusion, we've got to agree to let him go.'

'And we want you to go with him.' The

colonel looked anxious. 'Will you?'

I nodded. I was now a nursemaid to a ghost.

* * *

At first things were a little stiff. The professor liked me, yes, but he was not used to having me around. I knew that the first thing to do was to break down the barriers of his isolation and, the way I did it, was to make friends with Ginney.

She was ten years old, a cute youngster with long, plaited hair, a freckled face, and cheeky blue eyes. She had been around quite a bit, was full of the devil, and loved fun. She also liked plenty of conversation.

She had also been dead for six months.

It wasn't easy to make friends with a ghost. I studied her photograph until I saw her in my sleep. I watched the professor until I knew just how she must look to him. I made myself imagine her, talk to her, listen to her answers and then talk some more. I memorised her history so that we'd have points in common, and all the time I had to guard against a single slip, which would have destroyed the professor's trust in me. That, in itself, wasn't too important, but I dared not injure his belief in his delusion. It was the only thing that kept him sane.

I passed the major hurdle one night in a little hotel near the border. We had been travelling south because, as the professor said, Ginney needed the sun. I shared a room with the professor, I had booked another for Ginney, and he was getting her ready for bed. I had watched the play a dozen times, the undressing and putting on of the nightclothes. The undoing of the ribbons and the brushing of the hair. I sat and watched as his hands, thin with thick blue veins, the fingers long and sensitive, clutched the invisible handle and brushed the invisible hair. I leaned forward.

'Let me do that.'

'You?' He hesitated, a flicker of doubt in his eyes.

'Yes.' I grinned. 'You don't mind me brushing your hair, do you, Ginney?' I pretended to listen, then snorted. 'Of course I won't hurt you. Why, I brush my own hair every day.' I grinned at empty air. 'Look, tell you what I'll do. If I catch a snag I'll tell you a bedtime story. Right?'

I listened, nodded, then stretched out my hand for the brush.

For a moment I thought that it wouldn't work. The Professor hesitated, moving his hand beyond my reach, the doubt growing in his eyes.

Then, very slowly, he moved his hand back towards me.

I took the brush from his hand. I caught hold of Ginney and made her stand in front of me. I turned her and, carefully, I began to brush her hair.

It was the hardest thing I have ever done.

Because it wasn't enough to play-act. I had to really brush the hair of a real girl and that meant it wasn't enough just to pass the brush through air. I had to turn it, to drag it, to move in on the same plane, to avoid snags and to follow the contours of a head. I had to do that and, at the same time, control the wriggling of a cheeky ten-year old.

I had to do all this while being watched

by a man who had based his sanity on a delusion, which I was helping to maintain. I had to do a good job.

I was soaking with sweat by the time I had brushed the hair and my hands were trembling with strain. But I hadn't yet finished.

'*You caught a snag,*' said Ginney in my mind.

'I'm sorry,' I said aloud. 'I didn't mean it.'

'*You promised me a story.*'

'I know and I'll tell you one.' Deliberately I put down the brush.

'Go and kiss your daddy goodnight.' I waited while the professor bent his head then waited just long enough for her to return to me.

I rose, stooped, picked her up and carried her towards the door. I opened it, awkwardly as a man would who carried a child, closed it and then, because I daren't for one moment relax from the pretence, carried her towards the bedroom, drew back the covers, tucked her in and sat down on the edge of the bed.

Almost I yielded then. Almost. But a

sound, it may have only been the creaking of a floorboard or it may have been the professor following me, urged me to continue. So, sitting in the darkness, I told the story of the *Three Bears*, then *Red Riding Hood*, and then, just to make certain, the one about *Mother Goose*.

When I left that room I wanted a drink more than anything else in the world.

But I had something to do first.

The professor was working when I rejoined him. He sat at the table and covered sheet after sheet of paper with abstruse mathematical symbols. The floor was littered with discarded sheets, each one of which I would have to gather and destroy. He smiled at me and laid down his pencil.

'Ginney asleep?'

'Like a top.' I lit a cigarette. 'You've a fine girl there, professor.'

'I know it, Tom.' It was the first time that he had used my Christian name. 'I'm glad that she's taken to you.' He stared down at his hands and sighed. 'I'm really too old for her. Married late, you know, and missed the best part of life. I do my best but Ginney's young and needs young people around her.' He sighed again. 'It isn't easy.'

I wasn't quite sure what he meant so didn't say anything.

'Funny,' he poked at the heap of papers. 'I feel as if I can really get down to it now. You know what all this is about?'

'No.' I was deliberately casual and meant it. I didn't want to know. I could see that he wanted to talk but my job was to keep him working and he wasn't going to do that while I stayed. So I yawned stretched, and made for the door.

I heard the rustle of paper as I closed it behind me.

* * *

Cottrell was waiting at the rendezvous. He didn't say anything as I got into the car but he had a bottle and I consoled myself as he drove to the edge of town. There he halted and, with the motor running, we talked.

'Any luck?'

'He's working,' I said. I wasn't worried about leaving him alone. The entire area was lousy with Security men who would make sure that no one approached him but me. They must have had a hell of a job. Cottrell reached for the bottle, tilted it, then passed it back.

'How did you manage it?'

I told him and he nodded.

'Good. You've earned his trust and he'll be dependant on you. A little more and you'll have him jumping through hoops. Making friends with his delusion was a bright idea. Don't forget the sympathy.'

I looked at him in the dash-lit darkness.

'You don't like me, do you?'

'I don't like what you're doing,' he said harshly, and I caught the gleam of his eyes as he faced me. 'I don't like what's being done to the professor. I'm a doctor of sorts, a doctor of the mind, and it's my job to heal. What would you think of a doctor who deliberately encouraged a malignant cancer in a man because it increased his I.Q.?'

'Doesn't that depend on what he does with his increased I.Q.?'

'Maybe.' He seemed torn between the desire to talk and caution against talking too much. Desire won. 'I'm sticking my neck out in saying this but I personally believe that the professor would be better off dead than the way he is. Oh, he's happy enough while he can retain his delusion, but what about when it ups and hits him in the face? Anything can do it, a stranger, an incident, any one of a thousand things and he'll realise that he's been living in a dream. Then . . . '

He made a gesture.

'The nut house?' He nodded. 'So what? Would he be any the worse off?'

'If you can't live with a thing,' said Cottrell tightly, 'you escape from it. The only way the professor can escape is by forgetting. The trouble is he can never forget enough. So he keeps on trying. They call it dementia praecox. It isn't nice.'

'Then isn't it better to let him keep his delusion?'

'Not if we want to save his mind.' He looked away from me, his fingers drumming on the wheel. 'Don't misunderstand me. With proper therapy he can be made to accept his loss and learn to live with it. He can be cured of his delusion and, mentally, he wouldn't be harmed. But that takes time, lots of time, and they won't give him the time. They want what he can do now. So they give him his dream until he's done the dirty work and then they'll drop him like a hot brick.' He must have sensed my disbelief.

'Why not? What better way to safeguard that knowledge than by letting the brain that discovered it lapse into total insanity? What possible good could he be then to any foreign power?'

'It's too dirty,' I said. 'We wouldn't do anything like that.'

'No?' He shrugged. 'I've talked too much and you could get me canned if you wanted to. But I'm a psychologist and I know what makes men tick. One man wouldn't do it. A group of men would. Split responsibility. Avoidance of guilt. Add Security, fear, expediency, patriotism, the natural desire to take the easy path and the even more natural desire to be top dog, and the professor doesn't stand a chance. You'll see.'

He engaged the gears and let in the clutch. He didn't speak on the way back and I had plenty of time to think. I did a lot of thinking too, not about what he had said, but about something quite different.

About Ginney.

* * *

It's funny how you can get used to a thing. Once you convince yourself that what you are doing is right then the rest seems to come automatically. Actors have a name for it. They call an actor who can really live the part a *darfstella*. Only such an actor doesn't really act at all. If he's supposed to be an old man, then he is an old man. He walks like one, talks like one, even thinks like one. It makes for wonderful acting but it's hard on the nerves. To do what I had to do I had to believe in a ghost. So I believed in it. I got so that I could really see Ginney, sense when she was near me, consider her in everything I did. I accepted the professor's delusion and, in so doing, it became my own.

We stayed at the hotel ten days and the

professor worked all the time. While he was working I took charge of Ginney, taking her out and showing her the town, It was a small town with a little old mission built during the Spanish occupation, the usual markets, the usual things for tourists to see. We saw them all, and, once I forgot to remember that I was acting like a lunatic, it became easy. There were snags, of course. There was the time when I bought two ice cream cones, one for me and one for Ginney. I passed it to her and, naturally, it fell to the ground. It was a mistake and I was lucky that the professor wasn't with me. I wasn't so lucky the time we all went out to eat.

Maybe Security had fallen down or maybe it was just one of those things, but the restaurant we chose was pretty busy and seats were at a premium. We had a table and three chairs, one for the professor, one for me and, of course, the other one for Ginney. We ordered, Ginney wasn't hungry so she just sat and watched, and while we were eating a man came up and started to sit down in the empty chair. I stopped him just in time.

'Sorry, mister, but that seat's taken.'

'Is it?' He looked at the empty place, then at the crowded floor, then back at the vacant seat. He was a big man, arrogant, and I could tell that he was going to argue. I rose and pulled him away just as he reached for the chair.

'I said that it's taken.'

'In a pig's eye it is. Look, mister. I'm hungry and I'm going to eat.' He reached for the back of the chair.

I thought of Cottrell and what he had said about the fragility of a delusion. I could have compromised. I could have asked Ginney to sit on my lap or done any of a dozen things to make the incident a logical outcome of a crowded restaurant. But I thought of the professor and how he would feel at seeing his little girl pushed around and I knew that I couldn't risk his beginning to ask himself questions. I pushed the man away.

It was a mistake. It was hot, he was bad tempered, and he didn't like being pushed. He swung at me, his fist driving low into my stomach, and I gagged as the air rushed out of my lungs. He grinned and drew back his fist to finish the job and I cursed my crippled leg as I tried to brace myself. It wasn't necessary. A waiter came rushing up, full of apologies, and caught the man by the arm. He didn't look strong but there must have been something in the way his fingers dug against the nerves because the man winced and allowed himself to be led to a suddenly vacant table. Security, of course, but that didn't make me feel any better.

The professor was very quiet for the remainder of the meal.

'You know, Tom,' he said over coffee and I was glad that he'd broken the silence, 'the world is full of nasty people.'

'That character?' I shrugged and lit a cigarette. 'Forget him.' I winked at Ginney, or rather I winked at the empty seat where she was supposed to be. The professor took no notice.

'Your leg,' he said. 'Pardon me if it's a delicate subject, but how did it happen?'

'Hit and run driver,' I lied curtly. 'I never did find out who it was.'

'Yes,' he said, and his knuckles went white as he gripped his cup. 'That's what

I mean. The world is full of murderers and criminals, people who would be better off dead. Sometimes I wish that something would happen so that they would all die.' I was surprised at the emotion in his voice. It was the first time I had ever seen him really angry, and he was, burning with that helpless kind of frustrated rage which makes you feel all sick and twisted inside. I tried to change the subject.

'Don't think about it, professor. It takes all kinds to make a world.' I blew a smoke ring towards Ginney. 'How's the work progressing?'

'Finished,' he said, but he didn't sound like a man glad to have ended a chore. You can have the final results tonight.' He smiled at my expression. 'That's what you want, isn't it? The last set of equations so that they can begin the tests for controllable fission of non-radioactive materials. Bigger and better bombs at a fraction of the cost. The fools!'

'Please!' I'd begun to sweat. I couldn't know who was listening but one thing I was sure of. This was information that I wasn't supposed to know about. I didn't want to know about it either. I crushed out my cigarette. 'Let's get out of here and go for a walk or something.'

'Yes,' he said and rose from the table. 'I'll give you the papers and tomorrow we'll leave. Will you buy a car? I want to drive myself for a change.'

I nodded and we left. It wasn't until after he had given me the wad of papers covered with their potential dynamite and I had passed them on to my contact that I began to get worried. Not about the information, that would be flown straight back to the laboratories where they were all ready to make the first tests. Not about the incident in the restaurant. Not even about the fact that we were leaving in the morning. But about Ginney.

The professor seemed to have forgotten all about her.

* * *

We left the hotel the next morning in a cheap coupé guaranteed to fall apart after ten thousand miles. I wasn't worried. The car, like the professor, like me, like Ginney, was expendable. As long as it did its job I couldn't complain. The professor drove, handling the wheel with a surprising skill, and I slumped in the seat behind him, my hat over my eyes and those eyes glancing from time to time at the rear view mirror. Somewhere behind us, a spurt of dust on the horizon, Cottrell was still on the job. He would stay on it until he received word that the tests had proved satisfactory and then he would move in and take over.

I didn't like to think of what would happen then.

Once I'd satisfied myself that the professor could handle the car I relaxed and busied myself with thoughts. I was still worried by the professor's lack of attention to his little girl. For the first time since I had been with him he hadn't kissed her goodnight. He hadn't asked after her this morning, either, though I had made a point of settling her in the dicky seat with the baggage and asking her whether or not she was comfortable. But the professor had seemed to have something else on his mind.

Strange about a delusion. I'd known others who had their own private belief and, to me, it had always seemed that they had a trick of justifying or rationalising away anything that tended to shatter it. Cottrell had said that the professor was different. He had warned me that a word could shatter it and I wanted to discover why. The answer was surprisingly simple.

It was me.

My interference, my bolstering of the delusion, my own play-acting so as to make a fantasy a concrete reality. I had taken over as nursemaid and, by so doing, I had relieved the professor of the need to adapt what wasn't to what was. I believed in Ginney, to me she was alive and so, to the professor, she was alive too. No need for him to convince himself any longer. He could sit back and watch me do all the little things he'd had to do and, naturally, just as a mother with a trusted nurse no longer worried about her child, so the professor had ceased to work at his delusion. Because, to him, it was nothing but the proven truth. I saw her, didn't I? I talked to her, played with her, protected her. So he had returned to work freed of his anxiety and left me with the burden. But if I let him down, if I showed him that I thought it was all stark lunacy and that I'd been acting with my tongue in my cheek in order to get him to work, then . . . ?

I straightened with a vague impression that something was wrong. I opened my eyes and something cold gripped my stomach as I stared at the speedometer We were going fast, too fast, but I didn't realize just how much too fast until I looked at the scenery

We were on a narrow road winding down the side of a succession of hills, which without any straining of the imagination, could have been called baby mountains. The road was bad and, to one side, it fell away towards the rocky bottom of a gorge. The car was slithering from side to side as the wheels strained to hold the loose surface of the road. Even as I watched we veered to the wrong side, sent dirt pluming over the edge, then drifted back towards the stony verge. And we were going faster all the time.

What I did then was dictated by instinct. I cut the ignition and hauled on the handbrake. I grabbed the wheel and jammed my foot against the gear lever so that it couldn't slip out. I hung on while the engine compression helped to slow the car and, while I clung to the wheel, I prayed. We stopped three inches from eternity.

'You were going too fast,' I said stupidly. 'You might have killed both of us.'

'I know,' he said, and his face was dripping with perspiration. 'I'm sorry.'

I took over the wheel. He didn't argue about it and neither did I. He was shaken but not anywhere near as badly as I was and I had the crazy impression that he was disappointed about something. I drove slowly after that, handling the car like a matron on her first time out on a public highway, and it wasn't until almost dark that we came to a village tucked away in the foothills. I stopped the car before an apology of a hotel and climbed stiffly from behind the wheel.

The proprietor was more dark than white but he made us welcome, and the native cooking blended with the wine as good cooking should. After the meal the professor excused himself and went up to bed. I saw him to his room then went back downstairs and sat on the veranda, smoking, thinking, and waiting for Cottrell to catch up. Something must have delayed him because it was almost midnight before he arrived.

'What happened?' He was hot and tired and annoyed. 'It's a miracle I found you. You left the main road and buried yourself in these hills. I almost went over the edge twice following your trail.'

'I know.' I told him what had happened and his face went white.

'Are you sure?'

'You think that I could ever forget?' I dropped my cigarette and lit another. A moth, a wide-winged thing came fluttering towards the match and I knocked it away. 'I tell you he almost killed both of us. Hell! If I hadn't grabbed the wheel we'd have both been mincemeat.'

'And after you stopped the car, what then?'

'I told him he was driving too fast and took over.'

'Anything else?' He glared his impatience. 'Did you say anything, do anything?'

I frowned, trying to remember. 'No. I said that he was driving too fast and could have killed the both of us. He agreed and apologised. I — ' I broke off, staring at his expression. 'What's the matter?'

'Both of us,' he repeated sickly. '*Both* of us!'

And then it hit me right smack in the face. I'd totally ignored Ginney — and so had the professor.

'The death wish,' said Cottrell. 'He wanted to die but has the normal indoctrination against conscious suicide. Subconsciously he tried to commit self-destruction by driving so fast down that trail that an accident was certain. You stopped him just in time. But why should he want to die? Why?' He frowned as he thought about it. 'Did you do anything, say anything, to shatter his delusion?'

'Not that I know of.' I told him of the incident in the restaurant. 'It's a funny thing though, he didn't seem to pay any attention to Ginney afterwards. I thought that it was because he'd left it to me.'

'Maybe, or it could be that something reminded him that she was dead.' He looked even more worried. 'He gave you the finished work after that, didn't he?'

'Yes.' I stared at the tip of my cigarette and felt as guilty as hell. Because I'd remembered something. I'd remembered the way he looked when I'd lied about my accident. If he liked me, and I was sure that he did, then that was just one more black mark against humanity. Or the coincidence may have reminded him of what had happened to Ginney. 'Is it important?'

'I don't know. It's too late now anyway, the papers have arrived by now and they'll be hard at work making the tests.' Cottrell seemed more worried than ever. 'I don't like it. I don't like the way he tried to kill himself.' He rose to his feet. 'I want to see the professor.'

* * *

It was very quiet upstairs. The proprietor had gone to bed like an honest man and we seemed to be the only living things in the entire world. I led the way, favouring my bad leg, and striking matches to guide Cottrell. We heard the voice just as I opened the door of the professor's room. Cottrell gripped my arm just as I was about to call out and we stood there, alone in the darkness, listening.

'Ginney . . . Ginney . . . Ginney.' A mutter and a restless movement on the bed. ' . . . with you soon, darling. We'll all be with you soon . . . me . . . mummy . . . Tom . . . you like Tom don't you?' I started to say something and then changed my mind. ' . . . world's rotten, darling. Murderers . . . criminals . . . fools . . . all rotten. Better dead . . . all dead . . . all the same . . . all together . . . '

I stepped forward and almost cried out with the pain in my arm. Cottrell gripped me without knowing what he was doing, and, after I had pulled him back into the passage and lit a match, I could see his face ghastly white and shining with sweat. He didn't speak until we were back downstairs and even then he said nothing until he'd burned his throat with straight tequila.

'You can't fool the subconscious,' he said grimly. 'You can fool the conscious but that's all. He,' a jerk of the thumb told me who he meant, 'knows that Ginney is dead. He tried to deny that knowledge and we, God forgive us, helped him do it. But deep down inside he knew that she had gone for good.' He saw my expression and remembered that I was no psychologist.

'The professor is an intelligent man,' he explained. 'To remain intelligent his mind had to be efficient, and how efficient is a mind clouded with delusion? You took from him the need of maintaining that delusion and so he could finish his work, But, once you had done that, he had time to be objective. He could see you as others saw him and somehow he must have realized the futility of trying to resurrect the past.' He sighed. 'In other words he was on the road to a cure. But there was something else. They never found out who killed his daughter, and he wanted revenge. They never found out, so you said, who injured you, and you are his friend. He wants to be with his daughter and the only way he can do that is to die. But he can't commit conscious suicide. Conflict, Tom! Conflict leading to insanity and the desperate need to find an escape from opposed problems.

'And this is the man who has worked out the means to create fission in non-radioactive materials!'

* * *

I'm not stupid and I don't need a drawing but just now I wish I was a moron, or a moth, or something brainless and not tormented with thoughts of what-might-be. Cottrell has gone, driving like a madman over those rutted trails but he knows and I know that he can't possibly be in time. So I sit, smoking, thinking, listening to the cicadas and waiting for dawn.

Maybe Cottrell is all wrong, and the

professor has worked out a safe formula. Or maybe Cottrell is right and the professor wants the world to go up in atomic flame so that he can pay out the killer of his daughter and at the same time be with her in the only way he can.

5

Fallen Angel

A flash of rose, a scent, a voice which echoed in the hollows of his mind and, suddenly, he was alive again. Fully alive, really alive not lying on a slab while instruments probed and delved, measured and indexed, twisted and tested. Not writhing in torment as muscle and nerve and sinew were strained to the limits of endurance and then pushed further beyond. Alive and well and soon to be free. Free!

The concept was intoxicating as the drink and drugs he had once known which had rotted his brain and body in return for a brief euphoria. He sat and thought about it in the place where he was kept. A mist swirled about the area moulding itself into the illusion that he sat on a bench of stone, in a chamber of stone scented with the perfume of hidden blooms. Soon now, he would see real flowers, walk again in sunlight, feel the wind, the rain, the touch of snow. To eat genuine food, talk to real people, forget what had happened if forgetting was possible.

'It is.' said the alien. 'Most things are.' He had appeared as he always did, abruptly, seated, a tall, lean, white-haired man looking, in his simple robe, like an ancient Greek philosopher. It was a façade. An illusion to mask the true shape of the creature. 'But no interference on our part will be necessary,' he continued. 'Your race has a peculiar ability to ignore the unpleasant. The defensive application of a highly selective memory.'

'Yes,' said Frank. He could believe it. Once he had seen the creature as it really was. Now it was almost impossible to accept that such a thing could actually exist. 'I was told that I was to be released. Am I?'

'Of course, Mr. Engel. We do not lie.' The classical features creased into a smile. 'You probably feared that we would eliminate you but we have no reason for that. You may not realize it but we have much to thank you for. You have been most co-operative. With your assistance we have gained much knowledge of your world and we shall learn more. We are grateful.'

Grateful! Would a fisherman talk that way to a creature he had hauled from the water, cut open, looked at, sewn up and was ready to throw back into the sea? Maybe if the fish could talk but would he give it a reward?

'It is our custom,' said the alien. The words echoed without vibration, a soft tingling impinging directly on the cortex. 'Our ethics forbid us to take without giving something in return. The device is one much used among us for social convenience. It is an eraser. With it you can undo a mistake. Gain the advantage of a second chance. Avoid unpleasant situations. You should find it most useful.'

'Sure,' said Frank. 'But — ' He broke off for the alien had gone, the room, the swirling mist and walls of apparent stone. He still sat but the bench was of wood.

The air carried the scent of visible flowers. There was sound; the sigh of wind, the rustle of leaves, the shouts of children at play. And, all around, the bright warmth of a summer sun.

Summer? It had been winter when he'd been taken, cold, hungry, dying, without a job, a home, a friend, a shred of hope. The way a man gets when the money runs out and the drink and the drugs and nothing is left but hunger, the pain of diseased lungs and the ravages of dissipation. He'd been a good specimen for the aliens. Who would miss him? Who would believe him? Who would he want to convince?

No one. He was cured and he knew it. No more addiction. No more disease. A good chance to make a fresh start. He knew what needed to be done and he had the alien's gift to help him do it.

He sat and looked at it, eyes narrowed against reflected sunshine. Beside him a man stirred in his sleep smelling of staleness but human because of it. Just one of the drifters who thronged the park. Across the graveled path another bench held three others, two old, one a kid with a waxen face and twitching hands. One of the men rose, stretched, headed down the path. Frank ignored him, concentrating on the gift.

It was a ring, the band thick, wide, raised in one part, a prominence that could be pressured by the impact of the adjoining finger. The jewel was a large, domed, ruby-like stone striated with what could have been a diffraction grating. Frank was a social failure but not an idiot and some things were obvious. The ring was more than an ornament but just what he didn't know. The alien hadn't explained. He examined it again, studying the protuberance. He pressed it.

Nothing happened.

Nothing, that is. Aside from the fact that the man who had risen from the facing bench and who had walked down the path was abruptly sitting on the bench again. As Frank watched he rose, stretched and walked away. The stud on the ring sank beneath the squeeze of his finger. Nothing happened. He waited, tried again — and the man was back on the bench. He rose, stretched, walked down the path exactly as he had done twice before. This time Frank let him go.

He knew now what the alien had given him.

He leaned back filled with the wonder of it. An eraser, the alien had said. A device for social convenience. A thing with which to undo a mistake and to gain another chance. It was something you could need to use quickly, easily, have close all the time. What could be more convenient than a ring? A very special kind of ring. A neat device, he thought, looking at it. Compact, ornamental, unobtrusive, probably everlasting.

A one-way time machine.

* * *

The main-line station housed a throng of travellers. Frank ignored them all as he concentrated on the large digital clock. The figures read 18.02. He activated the ring. The figures changed to 17.05 Fifty-seven seconds, the same as twice before. He made more experiments.

Activated the ring threw you back in time, but you had to wait fifty-seven seconds before it could be activated again. No accumulation. The stud could be kept depressed and there would be an automatic activation. Nothing you carried less than fifty-seven seconds in the past went back with you. It was all he needed to know.

The crossing lights were at red. Frank, distracted, stepped from the kerb directly into the path of a heavy truck. Brakes screamed, a woman, a man. A moment of panic then his finger closed and he was instantly back on the sidewalk heading towards the crossing. He checked with his watch. Fifty-seven seconds. Call it a minute. He paused, waited for the truck to pass, the lights to change to green.

A minute.

Not long? Try holding your breath that long. Try resting your rear on a hot stove for half that time. In a minute you can walk a hundred yards, run almost a quarter of a mile, fall three. You can conceive, die, get married. A minute is time enough for a lot of things.

Frank closed his hand and looked at the ring. Thinking. Take the classical situation. A couple, the man old, the woman young. You greet them, assume the woman is the old man's daughter, discover she is his wife. Loss of equanimity, and the generation of embarrassment. So activate and go back in time. Meet the couple again but now armed with knowledge. Politeness reigns. In any society such a device would be in demand.

But not for soothing an old man's ego. Not just for that.

Not when he had no job, nowhere to live, an ache for luxury in his belly and a yen for the good life in his soul. He had drawn on the experience of three decades of tough living to get a wristwatch and decent shoes and clothing. But he still needed money.

A liquor store shone down the street, a bright cavern filled with bottled dreams. Frank leaned close to the window, squinting against the lights, staring inside and checking what he saw. The place seemed deserted, the owner probably busy out back. A cash register stood on the counter flanked by stacked cans. He waited, counting seconds. A minute and a half and no sign of life. He activated, walked into the store, operated the cash register and took out a thin sheaf of bills. He was almost at the door when the owner appeared. A big, beefy man with a balding head and savage eyes. He came charging from a room at the rear shouting and waving a baseball bat.

'Hold it you! Move and I'll smash your head in!'

He meant it. Frank squeezed the ring — nothing happened. Nothing would happen until the time was up. He had to stall.

'Now listen,' he said. 'It's not like it seems. It's a publicity stunt, see? Just for advertising. You'll — '

'By God, the nerve of it!' The owner came closer, lifting the club, snarling his hate. 'A stinking thief walks in and robs the till, then gives you a load of mouth. I'll give you mouth! I'll give you a damned sight more than that!'

Frank squeezed his fingers keeping the

stud depressed as he dived to one side. The owner was fast. The club slammed against the edge of the door then followed him down. He felt and heard the crack of bone as it slammed against his knee. He rolled as it lifted for another blow — and he was leaning against the window the glass cool against his brow. He fought to control his breath. He was safe his knee uninjured, the store seemingly deserted.

Mopping sweat he felt the bloom of anger. The bastard had tried to kill him. To smash in his skull for the sake of a little cash. He would be lounging in his room, watching television, enjoying something to eat. He'd have a gimmick rigged to the door to signal when anyone came in. That, and maybe a mirror to watch the till. Nursing his club and aching to use it. The blood-crazed slob! He had it coming!

Again he entered the empty store and opened the register but this time, instead of heading for the door, snatched up a bottle and moved to the rear. As the owner appeared he swung at the balding skull. The bottle shattered into a mass of sparkling fragments mixed with a flood of wine, blood and spattered brain. He dropped the neck and scooped up the club. The shape of a wallet bulged the rear pocket of the dead man's jeans. He bent, dragged it free, flipped it open and saw a wad of bills. Straightening he thrust it into a pocket and strode towards the door. A looming shadow blocked the opening.

Quickly he rammed his foot against the panel.

'Sorry. We're closed.'

'I want a drink. I gotta have a drink.' The voice was a begging whine. 'I got money, see?' A hand lifted, waving a crumpled note. 'Just a bottle of something cheap.'

A lush and close to desperation. Frank recognized the danger. To lock him out was to invite curses, broken windows, unwanted attention. To let him in was to give him a view of murder.

He activated the ring and was standing by the till cash in his hand. Quickly he reached for a bottle and moved to the rear. This time he didn't smash in the owner's skull but swung hard and low at the belly and groin. He took the wallet from where he knew it would be. The club remained where it had fallen. He thrust the bottle into the hands of the lush at the door. Outside a cab halted at his signal.

'Where to?'

'A casino. A good one.' Frank relaxed against the cushions as the driver glided from the kerb. 'Waste no time, friend. I feel lucky.'

* * *

Luck, the fortuitous combination of favourable circumstances, but who needs luck when they know what will happen fifty-seven seconds in advance? Long enough for the dice to settle, the card to turn, the ball to drop. The winner to win. The ability to make quick, impulsive, apparently stupid last-second wagers against a seemingly sure thing. Frank rode high, a sure-fire winner.

In more ways than one.

He stretched, enjoying the shower, the impact of water driven at high pressure against hair and skin, massaging and stimulating as it tightened tissue and stung flesh into an exhilarating awareness. He turned a control and gasped as the water turned into a frigid goose-pimpling medium. A titillation as many things were now thanks to the alien gift and his own aptitude. He jerked the control back to hot, waited, then cut the spray and stepped from the shower drying himself on a fluffy towel.

'Frank, darling. Are you going to be much longer?'

A female voice with the peculiar intonation of the inbred upper classes; a member of the aristocracy by birth and a failed marriage. The Lady Jane Smyth-Connors was rich, decadent, bored and a problem.

'A moment, honey,' he called and dropped the towel. A mirror reflected a pleasing image. Money had improved on what the aliens had accomplished; cosmetic magic smoothing away accumulated blemishes, the scars of his early days. He'd worked hard to gain the physique of an athlete. He had been born with a pleasing face. Money had taken care of other things, his clothes, his accent, the education of his tastes. He had become a fringe-member of the jet-set. Rich. Handsome. Riding high. Saddled now with a crippled bird.

'Frank? Come to me!'

'Give me a moment.' He resisted the instinctive rush of anger at the tone, the command. She was arrogant and domineering but that had been obvious from the start. He had met her in a casino, recognizing the desperation of a woman who wanted to win but could only lose. Recognizing, too, an echo of what he had once been. The opportunity she presented. He had made a point of meeting her and she'd been attracted by his looks, figure and calculated attention. Now, invited to her home, perfectly aware of what was expected, he stood on the edge of respectable security.

The bathroom had a window. He parted the curtains and looked into the night. Way down low a scatter of lights carpeted the misty ground. London was a nice city. England a nice place. Very nice, especially to gamblers — no tax was levied on winnings. Here, more than anywhere else, high prizes were to be won. Not just money, that was for the plebeians, but make the right connections and every day would be Christmas.

'Frank!'

Fretful impatience and the imperious tone of one accustomed to instant obedience. The woman waited to be served. Sighing he entered the bedroom.

She was a little older than himself, tall with a peculiar angularity, giving the impression of an overgrown schoolgirl who should be wearing tweeds and wielding a hockey stick. The appearance was deceptive. Generations of inbreeding had done more than fashion the distribution of flesh and bone. It had developed a festering degeneracy. She was, he knew, almost clinically insane but, in her class, people were never insane only 'eccentric', never stupid only 'amusing', never spiteful, savage, vicious or cruel only 'thoughtless'.

He reached out and took her into his arms and kissed her with educated skill. He ran his hands over her body, silk rustling as it fell from her naked flesh. Gently he bit the base of her throat, harder, felt her tense, her negative reaction.

'No,' she snapped. 'I hate anyone doing that!'

One bad mark. He counted seconds as he reached for the light switch. With darkness she squirmed, pushed herself free of his embrace.

'I hate the dark! Must you be like all the others?'

Two bad marks. Twenty seconds to go. Time for one more exploration. His hands reached out, made contact, moved with studied determination. She sighed with mounting pleasure.

'Frank — my angel!'

He activated the ring.

Reaching out he took her in his arms this time making no attempt to nibble or bite. Her clothing rustled to the floor and her skin gleamed with a nacreous sheen. He looked at her with bold admiration and his hands moved in the way he had learned gave her pleasure.

She closed her eyes, fingernails digging

into his back. 'Talk to me,' she demanded. 'Talk to me!'

He began counting seconds.

Later, as she lay in satiated slumber, he rested, thinking, planning, oddly amused. He had been the perfect lover. He had said and done all the things she had wanted in the exact order she had wanted them and most important, without her having to instruct him at any time. He had been a reflection, an echo of her complex needs, and why not? He had worked hard to map the blueprint of her desire. Exploring, investigating, erasing all false starts and mistakes. Doing and saying nothing that had been unwelcome.

What else could he be for her but perfect?

He turned, looking down at the woman, seeing her not just as flesh and blood but as a soul in desperate need. A mass of conflicting emotions and frustrated needs, one not to be used but to be helped.

She sighed, opened her eyes, looked up at the face of her lover. 'My angel! My darling!'

He said what she wanted him to say.

She sighed again, same sound, different meaning. 'I've never been so happy. I can't believe this is happening.' Her fingers trailed over his arm, his hand, halted at the ring. 'Why do you wear this? It's so big. So heavy. It looks like a knuckle-duster. Is it for protection?'

'In a way.'

'I'll protect you,' she said, then added, musingly: 'Your name suits you. Engel, that's German for angel. Frank means honest. You are a frank angel. Are you an honest one?'

'I try to be.'

'Then I'll give you a treat. Tonight I'll take you to a party. You'll love it. There will be people it will help you to meet and all sorts of things to amuse you.'

Drugs and drink and he could guess the rest. 'No.'

'Why not? Don't be so staid, darling. Everyone needs to relax at times. We'll take a trip into paradise.'

'No,' he said again and added, 'I can't stop you doing what you want but I've been where you're heading for and I don't recommend it. Anyway, I can't see you tonight.'

'Why not?' Jealousy reared her upright. 'I need you. You know that. Why can't I see you? You said — '

'I know what I said and I meant every word of it. I love you to distraction, darling, but I have to fly to New York. Business,' he added. 'After all I do have to make a living.'

She said, quickly, 'You don't have to worry about that, darling. I'll speak to Daddy and — '

He closed her lips with his own. 'I still have to go to New York,' he insisted. Against her naked body his hands did what she wanted them to do. 'And later, after I return — '

'We'll get married,' she said. 'I never want to lose you.'

Christmas, he thought, as dawn paled the sky.

* * *

The plane was big, sleek, beautiful with matching flight attendants all breasts and legs and eyes and silken hair with a 'you may look at me because I'm beautiful but you must never, ever touch' attitude. A machine offering the ultimate in comfort for those willing to pay for it. Frank was willing and able and travelled luxury class. Room for everyone with plenty to spare and he was glad of it.

He felt tired. The night had been hectic and the morning little better. It was good to sit and relax neatly strapped in a form-fitting chair as the jets gulped air and spewed it behind in a man-made hurricane which sent the plane down the runway and up into the air. London fell away, a misty blur, the clouds dropped like tufts of dirty cotton and then there was only the sun, a watchful eye in an immense iris of blue.

He liked to travel and a little absence could make a heart grow fonder and, for him, there was a kick in flying. He liked to look down and think of all the emptiness between him and the ground. Felt his stomach tighten with acrophobia, the delicious sensation of fear experienced in perfect safety. Height had no meaning on a plane. All you had to do was to look straight ahead and you could be in a train. A Pullman, naturally, nothing but the best was good enough for the winners in this world.

And he was one of them. Wealthy and soon to be married to a rich and doting woman who had all the right connections. One for whom he felt an unexpected fondness. He would be fair taking nothing she wasn't willing to give. He didn't have to. Not if what he planned worked out.

He unstrapped, stretched his legs, glanced through a window as the captain's voice came over the speakers telling anyone interested of their height and velocity. Through the pane he could see very little. The sky, the clouds below, the tip of a wing. Old stuff. The blonde attendant was far from that. She swayed among the seats, caught his eye, responded with instant attention. Was he quite comfortable? Would he like a pillow? A newspaper? A magazine? Something to drink?

'Brandy,' he said. 'With ice and soda.'

He sat on an inner seat close to the wall of the cabin so that she had to step from the aisle in order to lower the flap and set down his drink. He lifted his left hand and touching her knee, slid his palm slowly up the inside of her thigh. He felt her stiffen and saw the expression on her face, a compound of incredulity, outrage, interest and speculation. Automatically he counted the seconds. Fifty-four . . . five . . . six . . .

He pressed the stud on his ring.

The tray made a little thudding sound as it came to rest, the brandy a liquid gurgling as it gushed from the miniature bottle over the ice. She smiled, gesturing with the punctured can of soda. 'All of it, sir?'

He nodded, watching as she poured, remembering the soft warmth of her thigh, the yielding temptation of her flesh. Knowing he had touched her only because it was forbidden. A stupid, childish thing to have done and totally unnecessary. If he wanted her she was available, her body language had made that clear. Did she know what he had done? No, he decided as she moved away. To her nothing had happened. She had served him a drink and that was all. But — ?

Brooding he stared at the ring. You activated it and went back fifty-seven seconds in time. All you had done during that period was erased. You could do anything you liked and none of it mattered because it had all been cancelled. But it had been real. He remembered the pulped skull of the liquor store owner. A murder cancelled but it had happened. He could remember it.

Could you remember what had never taken place?

'Sir?' The stewardess was back, smiling, some magazines in her hand. 'I thought these might interest you,' she said. 'I picked a range. Would you care for another drink? The same as before? Right away, sir.'

She gave it to him and swayed across the cabin as he reached for the magazines. Naked women ogled at him from the pages of a soft-porn publication and he wondered why she had chosen it. To hint that she was far from being a prude?

To arouse his interest?

To test his sexuality? His interest? Checking him out in her own way as he had done Jane the previous night. But he had no interest in pictured nudity.

The magazine fell to one side as he reached for a different publication. One dealing with oddities of nature and science and strong on the occult. He flipped pages, pausing to read, interested despite his cynicism. One article in particular held his attention.

According to the author some fifteen million Americans claimed to have been abducted by aliens, tested, interfered with, examined and then released with only the vaguest of memories of what they claimed had happened.

So he was not alone.

Yet if he could remember why couldn't they? Had their experience been based on nothing but mass hysteria? Wishful thinking? A simple desire to break out of faceless conformity. Had each received a gift? Could they be recognized by the rings they could be wearing?

He looked at his own knowing it was

not what it seemed. But was it more? He leaned back, thinking, remembering the calm figure in the simple robe. The explanation he had been given. Closing his eyes he made a mental journey back in time, feeling the stone of the bench, the flower-scented mist. Seeing the figure dressed in a simple robe, the alien resembling an ancient Greek philosopher. What had he said?

'You may not realize it, Mr. Engel, but we have much to thank you for. You have been most co-operative. With your assistance we have gained much knowledge of your world and we shall learn more.'

Learn more? How?

The ring — it had to be the ring. It swelled in his vision the stone a baleful eye. A time machine — but what else? A recorder? A transmitter? A tracking device? Had it monitored each activation? Was it a continuation of his physical examination? A means to test his moral fibre? Turning him into a representative sample of what could be expected from any of his species?

If so they would learn how strong

curiosity was to the human race. How tempting wealth and power. His business in New York was to meet experts in computer technology and other fields. Those who could scan the ring with specialized techniques, testing, prying, monitoring in order to determine the composition of the metal, the stone, its design and molecular structure. If it could be copied he would gain wealth beyond the dreams of avarice.

And he would have given freedom to the teeming inhabitants of an increasingly violent world. A defence against attack and injury. A means of escape from disasters and unthinking acts of violence. Had the aliens guessed what he intended?

He lifted his hand and stared into the stone. The ring was his to do with as he pleased. A gift. A thing given him by something resembling an ancient Greek and he remembered a cogent statement learned when young. 'Beware the Greeks when they come bearing gifts.'

But not this one. It had given him stature. The chance of social enhancement. Of confirmed social security but it could give him what he still lacked, the unquestioning power of incredible wealth.

The plane rocked a little. The voice from the speaker was calm, unhurried. 'Will all passengers please fasten their safety belts. We are heading into an area of minor turbulence. You may see a little lightning but there is absolutely nothing to worry about. We are, of course, flying well above the area of storm.'

The blonde came through the cabin, tutted when she saw his unfastened belt and made it fast. As she walked away he reached for the magazine, wondering if, in the letter column, there could be a claim from someone who had something concrete to show for their claimed meeting with aliens. The magazine fell from his lap to one side beyond his reach. Impatiently he released the safety belt and picked up the publication.

It held nothing of interest. Smiling at the stewardess he gestured for her to fetch him another drink.

Something hit the roof of the cabin. There was a ripping sound, a blast of air, an irresistible force that tore him from his seat and flung him into space. Air gushed from his lungs as he began to fall. He gulped, trying to breathe, to understand. Arctic chill numbed his flesh. He twisted, saw through streaming eyes the jagged gash in the fuselage, the shattered wreckage of the tail.

An accident, he thought wildly. A fireball, a meteor, metal fatigue even. A crack in the cabin wall and internal pressure would do the rest. And now he was falling. Falling!

His fingers squeezed in frenzied reaction.

'Please, sir.' The blonde came towards him as he reared to his feet. 'You must remain seated with your safety belt fastened unless — '

'Listen!' He grabbed her by both arms. 'Tell the pilot to change course. Tell him now. Hurry!'

A fireball or meteor could be avoided. They would be safe if the course was changed fast enough. But it had to be done now. Now!

'Quick!' He ran towards the flight deck the girl at his heels. Damn the stupid bitch! Couldn't she understand? 'This is an emergency!' he shouted. 'Change course immediately!'

Something hit the roof of the cabin. The compartment ripped open, metal coiling like the peeled skin of a banana. The blonde vanished. The shriek of tearing metal was lost in the explosive gusting of escaping air. Desperately Frank clung to a seat. He felt his hands torn from the fabric, his body sucked towards the opening. Once again he was ejected into space to begin the long, stomach-wrenching five-mile fall.

'No!' he screamed his terror. 'Dear God, no!'

He activated.

'Please, sir, I really must insist! You must allow me to fasten your safety belt.'

He was standing by his seat and the blonde was showing signs of getting annoyed. Annoyed!

'This is important,' he said, fighting to remain calm. Ignoring the stares of the other passengers all neatly belted in their seats. 'In less than a minute this plane is going to fall apart. Do something about it!'

Why did she stand there looking so dumb?

'You stupid cow, get out of my way!' He pushed her to one side and lunged towards the flight deck. 'Change course!' he yelled. 'For God's sake — '

Something hit the roof of the cabin. Again the roar, the blast, the irresistible force. Something struck his head and blurred his senses. He activated and found himself still in the open gulping at rarefied air and shivering in the savage cold. To one side, far lower, the shattered plane hung in a cloud of dissipating wreckage. Tiny fragments hung around it; one of them, perhaps, the blonde.

Below the sea spread in a shimmer of light and water. His stomach constricted with the overwhelming terror of acrophobia as he stared at the waves. Imagining the moment of inevitable impact. Falling he would die ten thousand deaths in cringing anticipation.

Spasmodically he clamped his fingers tightly together against the ring. Immediately he was high in the air again with almost a minute of grace in which to fall.

Fifty-seven seconds . . . repeated . . . repeated . . . repeated . . . repeated . . . repeated . . .

Falling, endlessly falling.

An angel suspended between Heaven and Earth.

6

Sell Me a Dream

Often I think that market places are the most romantic spots in the world. Not your glistening palaces with their serried shelves and all their wares ranked in solid array; they have merely stolen the name to give them a grace they do not have. They are cold places, sterile with their boxes and bags all wrapped and sealed and carefully devoid of all interesting odours. They are soulless in their mechanical efficiency and immoral in the way they shamelessly cheat with their large, economy sized packages that contain two parts of produce to one part of air. They are mere vending machines, nothing more, and I will have none of them.

But the market places, the real market places, how wonderful they are! London is well supplied with them as is every large city and, forty years ago, there were more than there are now. Those were the days when naphtha flares beat back the night, casting a flickering, ruddy glow over the stalls loaded with fruit from foreign shores. Oranges and lemons, pomegranates and bananas, chestnuts in the winter together with great slabs of sticky dates, pressed, dried figs and muscatels, almonds and sweet walnuts. In the summer soft fruits from Kent and crisp lettuce, cucumbers, radishes and tender spring onions.

Those stalls have changed now. Together with the old staples other, even more exotic fruits have shouldered for themselves a place in the cramped display. Aubergines and peppers, uglis and lychees, fresh figs and the once luxurious mushroom, all have come to enchant the eye and tease the palate. But one thing has not changed.

In every market place you will find them. The stalls and corners heaped with apparent rubbish, the junk displays, the relics of a bygone age, once treasured and now tossed aside to this, their last resting place before final destruction. They fascinated me then as they fascinate me now, those stalls. Not so much for what they offer for sale as the questions and stories those articles hold. I used to spend hours wandering up and down, pausing by some interesting specimen, holding it in my hand, wondering at its past history, its past use, the care which went into its fabrication and the pleasure and pride it must once have given.

I was young then, and romantic, and still had to learn of the hard cynicism that the city instills into all who seek fame and fortune within the confines of its narrow streets. My work was hard, the hours long and I had little time and less money for pleasure. And so I, as many others have done, found what pleasure I could as cheaply as I could. And there is no entrance fee to the market places.

I became known after a while, and tolerated with that innate good humor which is a Londoner's birthright. I was chaffed a little and it would have been beyond the forbearance of flesh and blood to refrain from trying to sell, but my refusals were taken in good part and my presence at the stalls did no harm, did some good in a way for customers will always gather where there is apparently another of their own kind.

Loneliness was my companion then as it has been all my life and, inevitably, I sought escape from monotony and dull routine in the realm of books. I was catholic in my taste, reading avidly any and all tales of adventure, romance and fables of foreign lands. My reading did not detract from the pleasure I found in the market places, rather it added to it, so that I would stand, with, perhaps, an old, battered telescope in my hand, a half of a spectacle frame or a carved oaken toilet box, my thoughts winging wild flights of imagination.

Was this telescope used at Trafalgar? Did some sea-dog lift it to his eye to stare at some scudding sail? Were those dents the result of war, the thunder of the guns and the crash of round-shot splintering the masts and scuppers of some long-vanished ship of the line? Did that spectacle frame once rest on the ears of some noted wit of an age when wit was the essence of social conversation? Had some perfumed dandy kept his pearl studs in that box and, if so, why had it passed from hand to hand to reach this, its final resting place? Had there been a duel, pistols for two and coffee for one or, perhaps, the flash of small swords in a dew-wet park?

Wild speculations and yet they amused me and lifted my thoughts from the common round. And, in all my searching, admit it or not, there was the hint of even wilder adventure. I had been reading the *Arabian Nights* and kindred stories and my head was filled with tales of magic Djinn, strange lamps, Seals of Solomon and all the myth and fable of an unreal world. Other stories, too, had fired my imagination, tales of strange things being found in strange shops, articles which all unknown to the vendor, held unusual powers.

It would be nice, I thought, to stumble across such a treasure in my wanderings around the stalls of the market places. Impossible, of course, but, hope being what it is and youthful imagination as strong is it was, desire led my common sense into a winding, mist-filled path. So it was that I took to rubbing every foreign-seeming object and muttering some half-shamed command as I rubbed. Brasses from India, probably manufactured in Sheffield, were my prime subjects. Then oddly shaped fragments whose purpose had become lost in time. I was self-conscious about it and yet, so strong was my conviction that such things had once happened and could well happen again, that I could not resist my search for an object that would contain more than it seemed.

And, incredibly, I found it.

* * *

I did not know then and I do not know now exactly what it was that I found. I can guess of course, and speculate and toy with fantastic imageries but I do not *know*. And I shall never know, not for certain and never without a shred of sneaking doubt. But I believe now, as I did not suspect then, that I had found Paradise . . .

In shape it was a flattened ovoid roughly three inches in diameter and about half as thick in the centre, tapering to a rounded edge. It looked like a sea-washed stone and yet, despite that initial appearance, it held within itself, either because of shape or substance, something that attracted both hand and eye. There was a feel about it, a sensation impossible to describe but oddly alien to the touch. It was a long time before I decided that the sensation was partly due to it not appearing to have any temperature but that was only a part of the reason; the true reason I never did discover.

I studied it, turning it over and over in my hands, searching for some flaw in the smooth surface and it was with a mounting excitement that I discovered that the surface at which I gazed was not its true surface at all. Somehow, either because of heat or pressure or, perhaps, by the design of some previous owner, the object had been coated with a rock-hard sediment of unglazed clay. Time and stress had flawed the covering so that it presented a false impression. It was smooth, yes, but that smoothness was superficial. As I stared I could discover a multitude of tiny lines, a microscopic network as if minute spiders had covered it with the delicate tracery of their webs.

It was not easy to disguise my excitement, harder still to put down the object, to lift other fragments of the displayed rubbish and to casually, seemingly as if by afterthought, to return to the rounded stone. It was a normal practice, the usual sparring of those who wished to buy from those who had to sell, but I was an amateur at the game and I deluded no one but myself.

Even so the thing was cheap. To the vendor it was a stone, nothing more, a scrap of rubbish he had collected together with other litter, but he lauded it before asking his price and shrugged when I demurred and offered a little less. So I paid his price and he must have thought me a fool to squander coppers on such a useless thing.

Coppers, when, as I know now, the thing was of a value beyond price.

But that was forty years ago and wisdom, for me, still waited in the future.

My first task was to attempt to clean my new possession. I examined it carefully with a borrowed glass and, with the point of a needle, prised and dug at one of the minute lines. I acted with exaggerated care, I did not want to damage it in any way through my ignorance but, as I probed, a tiny fragment of heat-dried clay came free revealing something beneath. Then I rested while I considered what to do next.

The thing had a coating, of that I was sure, but how to remove it without doing harm was not so clear. In the end I compromised and, filling a saucepan with water, set it to boil and immersed within the bubbling liquid the stone I had purchased. It was, I realize now, a forlorn thing to do. Water will not soften heat-dried clay; I might as well have tried to boil a brick into its virgin materials, but I was ignorant and impatient and used what materials I had to hand. Even so I finally began to despair. For hours I boiled the object, replenishing the water when it was necessary and squandering more coppers on further supplies of gas and, when my patience was exhausted, I lifted the stone from the saucepan and rested it on my tiny table. With glass and needle I sat ready to attack the coating once more and it was then that I discovered one of the peculiarities of the stone. It had no temperature.

I had thought that it would be too hot to touch and logic was with me on that assumption. It had been immersed for hours in boiling water and should, by now, be as hot as boiling water. It wasn't — it was as when I had first touched it, strangely cool to the hand. It was while I sat considering this strangeness that I noticed that the clay-like coating was crumbling from the surface beneath.

Crumbling, not flowing or falling, but crumbling as if it yielded to pressure from beneath. Excitedly I picked up the ovoid and wiped it free of the last traces of the stuff that had covered it and then, entranced, sat and stared at what I held in my hand.

It was a jewel; somehow I never doubted that. It was smaller now — the substance covering it had been a quarter of an inch in thickness — and it rested on my palm, cool and with very little weight. It was smooth and with the slickness of glass or of ice, of a peculiar granulated consistency, translucent and yet fogged so that the eye seemed to stare into limpid depths only to be baffled by inner walls of opacity. It was like staring into impact-shattered ice or layers of frosted glass but it was more than that for the eye was not repelled but attracted and it seemed to me, staring into the ovoid, that if I could but concentrate a little more, stare a little harder, then I would be able to peer into the heart of the misty dimness.

And, somehow, I wanted to do that, wanted to do it with every fibre of my being. To me, at that moment, nothing was so important than that I should stare into the heart of the stone. And so it was that I discovered the light within.

The stone was hollow, subconsciously I must have realized that all along, nothing of its size and composition could have been so light had it been solid. But even so it came as a shock to discover that, buried within the depth of the ovoid, a tiny suggestion of light floated and drifted like a thistledown on a gentle breeze. It was small, so small and so dim that I would never have seen it had not darkness fallen while I had sat wrapped in contemplation and had my eyes not been strained to focus on so small an area.

Rising, I lit the gas and by its flaring light examined the stone again. Because of the brightness or because of my breaking of concentration, I could no longer see the tiny speck of dim radiance within the ovoid and, indeed, I no longer cared to look. Tiredness had come upon me with an unusual swiftness and sleep beckoned like an entrancing woman. I yawned, and yawned again and, after what seemed like a long time, managed to summon strength to undress and turn down my bed. Two things yet remained to be done, one obvious and the other illogical but, nonetheless, I did them both. I turned out the gas and, picking up the stone, slipped it beneath my pillow.

Why I should have done that I did not know. Perhaps it was the age-old instinct to guard a treasure or perhaps it was because of some deeper compulsion but, at the time, it seemed a perfectly natural thing to do.

And then I went to bed and fell asleep as soon as my head touched the pillow and, as soon as I closed my eyes, I dreamed.

I cannot describe that dream and, if I could, I would not. Some things are too personal for discussion, too intimate for anything but memory. I was young and poor and had few acquaintances and no friends. I lived in a cheap lodging and, as yet, I was a stranger to women. My days were a dull humdrum of monotonous routine with the prospect of promotion a tantalising wisp of promise and success to come. This was my life, my real life, but in my dream! Oh, God, in my dream!

I woke with memory surging in my head and felt almost a physical pain as I stared at the tiny square of un-curtained window and the rooftops outside. It took a little time for me to realize that was reality and that other, that glorious life, had been but a dream and, when realization came, the sting of tears dulled my eyes and I wished that I could turn and sleep again and lose myself forever in that wonderful world.

I did not. Habit is a stern taskmaster and my fear of unemployment was a very real one. And, I consoled myself, there would be other nights and, perhaps, I could dream the same dream again and again. It cheered me, that thought, so that the world seemed to be not so grim after all. Breakfast, poor and hurried though it was, cheered me even more for I was young and the young find it hard to be sad when well fed. It was only as I was opening the door that I remembered the stone.

Last night, without thought or logic, I had placed it beneath my pillow. Now, driven by the same impulse, I took it out and placed it on the window ledge so that the diffused rays of the sun would shine directly on it during the day. And then, suddenly conscious of the need for haste, I ran from my room and down the stairs and only just managed to reach my office in time.

It was the beginning of what was to become routine.

* * *

I had heard men talk of the power of dreams and had never fully grasped what they meant. I now know that they were talking of a different form of dream; that they were really talking of ambition, but the words they used and the claims they made found an echo in my heart. Dreams, to me, began to replace reality so that each day when my work was done I would hurry home, snatch a hurried meal and then, almost with reverence, would lift the stone down from its ledge, place it beneath my pillow and retire at once to bed.

It was a bad habit and it began to have its effect. Without any form of exercise I grew thin and weedy, my natural paleness turning into a sickly pallor. My concentration suffered, how could rows of figures interest me when, each night, I was wafted to a world of my own? And it became more and more difficult to reach work on time. Fortunately my pallor was misconstrued; my superiors thought that it was due to too much studying at night, and I gained a false reputation, which enhanced me in their eyes. My lateness, however, was more serious. Twice I arrived behind time and twice I was warned and, when about a month after I had first acquired the stone, I woke to hear the church bells tolling the hour and knew that I was already late, I felt despair.

Employers then were not as lenient as they are now and to be late again was to invite the threatened discharge. My only hope was to feign illness and this I did, sending a message by my landlady's son and then, sick with worry, settled down to spend the day as well as I might. Inevitably I examined the stone.

It fascinated me as it always had and now I had more cause for that fascination. The thing was alive, somehow I could sense that and, too, I sensed that it was the fount and cause of my dreams. Sitting with the ovoid poised in my hand,

I stared at it as another man in a different time might have stared at a holy relic. But, unlike such a man, my mind teemed with questions.

How had it come here? Who had made it? What was its purpose and why had it been so thickly covered with a substance foreign to its nature? If it was alive, then who or what had given it birth? I sat with my back to the window, the ovoid in my hand, and I pondered with what wisdom I possessed on something, which, I now know, I had no hope of understanding.

Holding it in shadow, as I was, the tiny light within the stone shone with an unaccustomed brightness. It moved with a strange, restless urgency, totally unlike the first drifting motion I had discovered. My dreams, too, had of late, taken on a new, disturbing quality. There was a poignant quality about them, a soul-wrenching impression of utter despair so that I woke with a dreadful unease and spent the day in a moody depression. There was something I felt that needed to be done, something that I had to do and, coupled with this, there was an overwhelming impression of nostalgia and a hopeless yearning for something I could not quite understand.

So must a prisoner feel, I thought, cooped and hampered in his cell, tormented by bright memories of what he had missed and was missing and, too, the fearful urgency of the sense of the passage of time, the terrible knowledge that, even were he to escape, it would be too late. I could not analyze these impressions, they were not clear enough for that and, too, I lacked the experience to recognize them for what they were. All I knew was that, more and more of late, I had woken from my dreams conscious of a thing which had to be done and which I should do. But what that thing was I did not know.

Now, staring at the ovoid, I began to guess. It was alive, the thing within, and, somehow, it had been imprisoned within the stone in my hand. I had fed it, all unknowingly perhaps and without that intention, but I had given it the strength it lacked. Heat, perhaps, the heat from the boiling water, which had easily penetrated these minute cracks on the outer covering, had, at first, awakened it. And I had rested it in the sunshine and so given it the radiant energy on which it survived.

Insane speculation? Perhaps, and yet a sick mind in a sick body drifts easily into fantasy. To me, sitting with my back to the window, the ovoid pulsed in shadow in my hand, staring at the tiny mote of darting light and with my being tormented with strange, unaccustomed, dream-induced emotions, it all seemed logical enough. It answered too, the reason for the outer coating. Some previous owner, a man of scientific bent, perhaps, had reasoned as I did now and, to safeguard himself from dreams, had insulated the thing from outside sources of radiant energy. And, thinking so, it seemed to me a cruel and monstrous thing to have done. It was like penning a singing bird in a too-small cage and there leaving it for the gross pleasure of those who found enjoyment in the pleading trills of a broken-hearted creature.

Yet a cage may easily be opened and I

could see no way to free the thing within the ovoid in my hand.

It was a new train of thought and it came to me without conscious volition. Never before had I thought of the possibility that the stone could be opened and yet, now that I thought about it, it seemed obvious enough. It had been made and sealed after making; therefore it should be possible to reverse the procedure. The possibility excited me so that I ignored the thin, warning voice deep in my heart. Did I really want to open the ovoid? Did I really want to loose what darted within? I had stumbled on a treasure equal to the Lamp of Aladdin for, though it could not give me material possessions, it could give me a world of my own beyond the wall of sleep. And a man can spend half his life, more if he tries, lost in sleep. It would be more than a fair exchange, this world of dreams for the world of reality. And what did the real world have to offer me in comparison with what I had tasted?

So evil must have whispered to Judas and, fool that I was, I prided myself on being stronger than he.

I opened the ovoid.

How even to this day I do not know. One moment I was turning it in my hands, my thoughts on freeing what lay imprisoned within, the next it lay in two hollow halves within my palms and, like a burning spark from some ancient fire, a mote of radiance darted past my head and out of the window and up and up into the infinite vastness of the sky. And I was left holding the broken ruin of what had been the most precious thing I was ever to know.

I was holding the broken shards of my life for, that night, I did not dream nor have I ever dreamed again.

Markets are wonderful places and part of their wonder is the people you meet. They walk slowly up and down, pausing at stalls heaped high with apparent rubbish and their hands pick and their eyes shadow as they stare at what they hold. Maybe they rub what is in their hand and mutter a little and that can be put down to the senility of age or the rash hope of youth. But the young do not deserve pity while the old deserve little else. So if you see an old man, bent now and with weak eyes peering through thick lenses, bearing the stamp of forty years of monotony and with a face almost devoid of hope, do not laugh at him as he picks and stares, examines and sighs, and turns away to try at some other stall.

He is only searching for a dream.

THE END

Books by E. C. Tubb
in the Linford Mystery Library:

ASSIGNMENT NEW YORK
THE POSSESSED
THE LIFE BUYER
DEAD WEIGHT
DEATH IS A DREAM
MOON BASE
FEAR OF STRANGERS
TIDE OF DEATH
FOOTSTEPS OF ANGELS
THE SPACE-BORN
SECRET OF THE TOWERS
THE PRICE OF FREEDOM
WORLD IN TORMENT
THE RESURRECTED MAN
THE GREEN HELIX
THE FREEDOM ARMY
JOURNEY INTO TERROR
ESCAPE INTO SPACE
THE LUCK MACHINE
SANDS OF DESTINY
THE WALL
GATH

FIFTY DAYS TO DOOM
THE DEATH ZONE
THE STELLAR LEGION
STARDEATH
TOYMAN
STARSLAVE
S.T.A.R. FLIGHT
TO DREAM AGAIN
THE WAGER
THE MING VASE

Other titles in the Linford Mystery Library:

SNAKE EYES

Richard Hoyt

John Denson, the Seattle private eye with his partner, Willie Prettybird — a shaman of the Cowlitz tribe — face their deadliest case: an engineered outbreak of anthrax in the Pacific Northwest. A ballooning list of suspects includes a rodeo cowboy; a barkeep with a roving eye; an ancient teacher at a high-school reunion — and the chief of police. Then there's the fund-raising televangelist Hamm Bonnerton. One of them is playing liar's dice, and coming up snake eyes. And killing people . . .

TERROR LOVE

Norman Lazenby

Married to Gilbert Brand, Kathryn imagines her marriage to be a happy one. It's studded with the parties of her husband's rich, socialite friends. But their attendance at a party given by his business associate, Victor Milo, tarnishes Brand's suave image. Kathryn discovers Brand attempting to strangle another guest, the nightclub singer Claudia, who becomes Kathryn's bitterest enemy. Then her world begins to crumble as she learns that Brand is an unscrupulous criminal . . . and she begins a descent into terror.

THE MING VASE

E. C. Tubb

Inside Cartwright House, a secret Government military project takes place. Men and women are well cared for, with every leisure facility. But they are prisoners, forbidden to leave. Their defection to, or capture by, foreign powers could be catastrophic. These people have very special powers, capable of being harnessed by enemies who could threaten and destroy western civilization. So when Klieger does escape, Special C.I.A. agent Don Gregson must find him. The only clue? Klieger has stolen a Ming Vase.

GHOST HOUSE

Gerald Verner

On holiday, Michael Wayland and his wife like the look of an empty house in a place called Bracken Bottom and decide to buy it. However, known as 'Ghost House', it has a sullied past — the previous owner was hanged for murder. Then, when Michael and his wife move in, odd things happen. A creaking gate is mysteriously oiled. And who is the strange man on the motorcycle — what is the message being flashed in the wood at night?